C000146639

The Half Term *B*reak

The Half Term Break

SUZANNE PARSONS

Copyright © 2014 by Suzanne Parsons.

Library of Congress Control Number: 2014905768
ISBN: Hardcover   978-1-4931-4262-0
                   Softcover   978-1-4931-4263-7
                   Ebook   978-1-4931-4264-4

All rights reserved. No part of this book may be reproduced or transmitted
in any form or by any means, electronic or mechanical, including
photocopying, recording, or by any information storage and retrieval
system, without permission in writing from the copyright owner.

This is a work of fiction. Names, characters, places and incidents either
are the product of the author's imagination or are used fictitiously, and
any resemblance to any actual persons, living or dead, events, or locales is
entirely coincidental.

This book was printed in the United States of America.

Rev. date: 03/24/2014

To order additional copies of this book, contact:
Xlibris LLC
0-800-056-3182
www.xlibrispublishing.co.uk
Orders@xlibrispublishing.co.uk
603413

Contents

Emily

Emily stood looking out of the kitchen window; she was silently smouldering inside. Why was her sister not reliable? It had always been like this; her sister, Tania, flitted in and out of their family's life, but it was down to Emily to do all the hard work. Even as a child, their parents spoilt Tania; even as a toddler, Tania often blamed Emily, even though Emily was three years younger. Once they got older, Tania even used to ask Emily to lie for her or to cover up for her. As a teenager, Tania was able to wrap her parents around her little finger; she was always able to look innocent whereas Emily would always look guilty. She could not stand still when being questioned by her parents. Tania used to get away with all kinds of things; some were petty—missing food from the fridge, broken toys, but some were more serious, and Emily got the blame for breaking the window in the greenhouse. But as they got older, Tania's crimes became more difficult to take the blame for— like being late home or late to college, drunk, flunking her tests and exams, dropping out of college when she became pregnant. Emily had also been blamed for stealing from her mother. Tania was beautiful with long blonde hair, big blue eyes—a typical eye candy. At eighteen, when Tania announced that she was pregnant, her parents spent a fortune on a big lavish wedding. Only a five-star country house was good enough for Tania. Tania didn't like her husband's family or his surname and insisted that she called herself Clifton-Peters once she was married. When Emily became pregnant a few months later at seventeen, her parents couldn't afford another lavish do, so Emily had a registry office wedding, and it was back to the garden for a cream tea reception. Emily always knew her parents felt guilty; right up to her death, her mum had tried to make it up to Emily. Emily knew that her parents had changed their wills and that she would be the main beneficiary, but Emily would have looked after her parents regardless. Emily loved her parents, and they had been so good to her.

Emily had taken on the brunt of the care of her parents when her mum was ill, and now a year on from her mum's death, she was the main carer for her father, although she preferred this to putting him in a home. She had two children to look after, plus her support teaching job at the local infant school, and this year because of the increase in children with special educational needs, she was basically working full-time. The only help she got was the day care centre. 'What would I do without this help?' she reflected. Her dad's pension paid for that, but as yet the family house was still his. Emily only wanted to sell it if she had to; that would be if her dad needed care in a residential home.

Her dad who had been diagnosed with Alzheimer's disease could no longer be relied upon to be safe in the house on his own, but she only put her dad in the centre during the day in term time. Dad liked his routine, but sometimes it could become very wearing, like Sunday afternoon.

Emily smiled to herself; looking back it was sweet really. Dad had always liked gardening; at his house, he had always had a vegetable patch and Mum had her flower beds. Every Sunday, they could be found outside in almost all kinds of weather, working together in their little garden, resting in one of the many little 'secret' havens that they had created, which had been great fun as a child to hide in.

On Sunday, her dad had decided that Emily's garden needed weeding, but he couldn't differentiate between a weed and a flower now. Emily had come outside with a cup of tea for them both to find her dad up to his knees in her flower bed, removing all her daffodils and fuchsias. Luckily, the daffodils were over and Emily had been able to salvage most of her fuchsias and replace them, but it had taken most of the evening, when she was already exhausted from cleaning, getting the house ready for her sister to stay. It was rare even now that Emily ever asked her sister for help, as she would always feel that she was asking for the earth and her sister was always so . . . Emily tried to think of the word to describe how her sister made her feel.

Emily turned suddenly when she heard the sound of a bowl dropping on the floor; her father looked at her, bemused. Emily forgot about her simmering animosity towards her sister.

'It's OK, Dad. We can clean it up.' Emily tried to keep the tiredness out of her voice; she knew that it upset her dad, when he thought she was cross with him.

As Emily cleared up the mess and soothed her dad, her thoughts wandered again. Not for the first time, Emily wondered how her mum had coped with her dad for the four and a half years previously to her death. Emily was now able to empathise with her mum and knew how hard it must have been for her, especially when she became ill herself.

Emily and Tania's mum had been a tower of strength when Emily's husband had decided that life at twenty-five years old, with a mortgage, two growing children, a wife, and a dog was not the life he wanted any more. Her mum had stepped up to help her with the two children, who at the time were only five and three years old so that Emily could go back to work and keep a roof over their heads.

That was six years ago before her precious dad was diagnosed with Alzheimer's disease, but her mum, true to form, had continued to look after the children until two years ago when she happened to mention to Emily over a coffee that she had found a lump in her breast. Emily and her mum used to go into town each Saturday morning whilst the children had swimming club. Mr Graham from next door would always pop round and sit with her dad on a Saturday morning, to give her mum a break once a week. Her mum would always bake him a cake as he had lost his own wife a few years ago. Her mum didn't drive, so they would do their weekly shopping and then have a coffee before returning to the leisure centre. Emily had quickly insisted that they visit the doctor and get it checked out, but it had taken a firm hold; it was not only her breast but secondary cancers; the doctors were not able to do more than offer palliative care.

Emily remembered only to well the fuss her sister had made when she was asked if she could come and stay and help look after their dad whilst their mother underwent treatment. She had not seemed worried about their mum's condition. She seemed to believe that everything would be OK. Tania lived in a bubble. 'Tania land' was how Emily's ex husband used to refer to her dismissal of 'real life'.

Tania had always led a sheltered life, where unpleasantness did not touch her.

Tania was three years older than Emily; at thirty-two, she was married to a city banker called Jim, short for James, which Tania insisted on calling him. But Emily had always acted older and taken on the responsibility and made excuse after excuse for Tania.

Tania's and James' lives were a complete contrast to the life that Emily and her children lived. Tania and her family lived in considerable luxury; their two children Adam, aged ten, and Grant, now thirteen, were at a private school and Tania's life was one big social whirl of golf, gym, and shopping, not at Tesco of course. Tania got her groceries delivered. No, when Tania went shopping, it was to designer stores, day trips to London or Oxford; she had even been known to hop on a plane and pop across to Paris, New York, or Rome for a shopping spree. A weekend away for Tania had to be Dubai, Monica, or Las Vegas; anywhere else she would think she was being asked to slum it. The last weekend that Emily could remember going away had been with her parents, and that had been down to Sidmouth in Devon three years ago.

Tania also loved lunches with the girls and holidays to some of the more exotic parts of the world, places that Emily knew she could only aspire to see. Some places she didn't even know existed, and she would get the children to look it up on the world atlas. Last time it was Goa.

Emily knew her sister was spoilt; her sister always thought that money could solve all problems. Hadn't her answer to the request to help with their parents just been to offer to foot the bill for the care that was needed to look after both their parents?

Hadn't she offered to pay to have their dad cared for in a home when their mother had died only nine months after she was diagnosed with breast cancer?

Emily bristled; this had not been the point. Both their parents had wanted to remain in their own home for as long as possible. It was a home that they had bought and lovingly cared for since they had married thirty-five years before, the home where they had brought up both their daughters. They had moved just outside Ringwood in the New Forest so that her dad could be able to take up his first teaching post, and they had built a beautiful garden and a home for Emily and Tania, where their friends were always welcomed.

When her mother was no longer able to care for her dad and had to go into respite care herself, Emily had brought her father to live with her.

That was a year ago, and today was the first time that she and her two children would be able to take a break, that was if her sister ever got here!

It was a two-hour drive from where her sister lived just outside London to the south coast, and she had rung three hours ago to say she was running late.

Emily had tried texting, but her texts went unanswered. Emily knew Tania had booked herself a hair appointment, "so what was the betting that she would still be in the salon?"

Emily suddenly shook herself out of her reverie. 'Come along, Dad. Let's take you into the lounge and you can start to watch the *Weakest Link*. You like Anne Robinson, don't you?'

Her dad stood up, grunting his reply, but Emily could see from his face that he recognised what she had said.

As her dad shuffled in front of her, Emily realised that he had wet himself again!

'Right, let's have a detour to the bathroom.' Emily remained calm, but the thought did pop into her head. 'How will Tania cope with this?'

Emily called up to both her children as she went, 'Grace, Max, have you changed your sheets yet? Your cousins won't want to slum it in your dirty laundry.'

'It's OK, Mum. We have nearly finished,' called down Max.

Max at nearly twelve was what could be called a typical teenager. It didn't worry him if his sheets never got changed, whereas their cousins would expect the rooms they would be staying in to meet the exacting standards of the best hotels in the world.

'Um, they are going to be disappointed,' thought Emily.

'Grace, have you done yours?' At nine years old, Grace was still going through the princess stage of her life and everything had to be pink and fluffy. Emily had given her one of Max's duvet covers to put on the bed, and she was hoping that when she went and checked she would have used this although it would not match her room.

Emily had made a special effort to decorate both her children's bedrooms last year when she knew she would be bringing her dad and turmoil to the house; she wanted to ensure that they both had space to go when they needed to and somewhere special to take their friends. She had also installed portable televisions with free view and DVD so that they could get to see their own programmes. They were brilliant with their granddad, but he loved game shows, and there were only so many that the two children could be expected to watch.

Emily helped her dad to change out of his wet jogging bottoms and underpants and thanked the day when Clare, the care worker at the day centre, suggested that this was a better option than the trousers that her dad had normally worn. It meant easier washing and no ironing, whereas the trousers always needed to be ironed, adding to the workload. Her dad had always been a smart man; he could always be seen working in his garden in a shirt and tie. Marie from the home carer's agency came in each morning to help Emily to get her dad up, showered, and dressed, ready for the mini bus to collect him and take him to the centre.

Once her dad was cleaned up and settled in front of the TV, she ascended the stairs to check on the children's progress.

Max looked as though he was only going away for a long weekend with just a large holdall and a rucksack, whereas Grace had packed a large holdall and rucksack plus a variety of other bags. Emily could see books and My Little Ponies sticking out.

When Emily entered Grace's room, she was able to see straight away that Grace had emptied her shelves and the windowsill of all her precious possessions.

Grace stood looking at her mother, waiting for a reaction, a look of slight defiance on her face, hands on hips. 'Well, I am not having Adam playing with my things. It's bad enough he has to sleep in my bed with one of Max's covers on my duvet. He is not touching my things.' Grace's voice was full of disgust.

Emily knew Grace had not forgiven her cousin for the time he had decided that her 'My Little Ponies' all needed to have their manes cut.

That was Christmas two years ago; Tania had invited Emily, Grace, Max, and their parents to stay for Christmas.

What a disaster that had been with Adam and Grant getting new Xboxes each and the latest games to go with them, whilst her two got much smaller gifts.

But her children played with their toys all during the festive period, whereas her nephews moaned around, complaining of being bored—that was until Adam decided to destroy the ponies.

True to form, Adam never got told off, but Jim or James came back on Boxing Day morning with a selection of whatever My Little Ponies ToysRUs had in stock.

Grace had hugged her uncle but would not forgive her cousin.

Suddenly, Emily heard a tooting in the driveway.

Quickly reassuring Grace that she would somehow get it all into their little Renault Clio, she ran down the stairs to greet her sister.

Tania got out of her car; well, actually she glided out of her car. Tania always glided. She was wearing what looked like very expensive designer trousers and top with her hair immaculately in place. It was proof of why Emily could not get hold of her; her nails were also manicured and looked as though they had just been done.

Emily did a quick double take as her sister seemed to have got another brand new car. This time it was a large four by four BMW Series X3 in the latest in colour of white. Parked next to her Clio, which was a 02 registration, it made it look small and shabby. The only saving grace was that Tania didn't like personal number plates. She had once said it was because people would not know she had a new car if they couldn't see the number plate. Today, Tania had a 2013 number plate.

Tania saw Emily give a quick look at the car. 'James had a large bonus from the bank,' she said in way of a justification of the fact that she had a new car nearly every year.

Emily looked at her sister and replied rather tartly, 'I thought the banks were in trouble.'

Ignoring the comment, Tania came round the car and gave Emily a hug. 'Darling,' her sister effused, 'the traffic was dire, so soz to be late.' She kissed Emily on both cheeks, well, air-kissed; somehow the entire gesture lacked any sincerity.

Just like normal, Emily heard herself saying that it was all OK and that she wasn't that late.

When Emily had gotten up that morning, she had intended to be on the way to Cornwall by 3 p.m., before the Friday holiday traffic; she had arranged to meet the lady of the cottage they were renting in the pub in the harbour at Port Isaac at 6.30 p.m. She had rung her ten minutes ago to apologise and explain. The lady who told her to call her 'Gwen' said that she could phone her when she got there and she would come down and meet them; at this rate, it would be ten o'clock when they arrived.

'Come on inside, all of you,' said Emily as she gave each of her nephews a hug.

'Grace, Max! Adam and Grant are here.' Two sets of feet thundered down the stairs, more excited at the prospect of setting off on their own holiday than actually seeing their cousins with whom they did not share a lot in common.

Emily took her sister through to the kitchen, and even though she would have loved to run out the door and jump into the car and make a start for the A31, she put the kettle on and made a pot of tea. Emily had remembered earlier in the week that her sister had kicked up a fuss last time she had popped down and Emily had made tea in a mug. So common! Emily had picked up a teapot that sat in a cup and saucer at the local garden centre.

'Take Adam and Grant upstairs and show them where they will be sleeping,' Emily suggested to her children who were hovering, waiting to be told to jump in the car.

'Dad is in the lounge watching Anne Robinson. He loves the programme,' she explained to her sister. Tania only quickly glanced towards the lounge door and made no effort to go in and say hello.

'Now I have filled the fridge with food that Dad likes and the basics like milk, bread, fruits, eggs, etc. His routine is on the door. There are numbers here for the doctor, nurse, the daily care agency, and the day centre, also the times that he goes to the centre. He gets picked up in a mini bus. I have also added my friend Wendy's number. She knows Dad well, and he responds to her. All his medication is written down, but I have put his medication out for you in this weekly box. Do not let Dad do it himself because he is now so forgetful that he is likely to take all three doses in one go.'

Tania looked at Emily, her eyes wide, reminding Emily of a rabbit caught in the headlights of her car when she went across the forest at night.

'What do you mean? More forgetful?' Not waiting for an answer, she carried on, 'I hope I will not have to be watching him every five minutes and I won't have to change him, will I?'

Emily started to worry about her own holiday slipping out of her reach, and she decided to do something that she did not normally do—lie.

'No, he is OK. Just don't want any accidents, do we?' Emily decided the best course of action was to make a quick getaway.

'Right, you have my mobile number if you really need me,' she said, putting the emphasis on really. 'Right, kids, are we ready?' The three of them quickly went and said goodbye to her dad, who was engrossed in the TV. She might as well have been popping to the shops. Emily had tried all week to explain that Tania was coming and they were going on holiday, but as the girls at the centre said, he didn't really understand any longer. They said if he did show signs of being upset they would reassure him. They had her number and would phone her if there were any major worries.

Both the children rushed out the door, pulling their bags behind them, and squeezed into the car, Grace sat in the back on her booster seat with her bags piled high around her. Emily knew that she would drop off to sleep before they reached the A31.

Max got into the front next to Emily to map-read; he had been poring over the map each evening the previous week, and they had written down the important towns on the journey so that he could trace the route. This was something that Emily and Tania had always done with their parents when they went down to Cornwall each year for their summer holiday.

As children, they had spent the majority of the six weeks' school holidays in North Cornwall. As her dad had been a teacher all his working life, he had the majority of the summer holidays off although he did take marking and other work with him to do in the evenings or on rainy days. Their mum didn't work when Emily and Tania were young; she took a small secretarial job once they started school, but this was a term-time only job so that she could be with the girls during their holidays. They had always owned a four-berth caravan, which periodically their parents would update. During other holidays, both Tania and Emily were allowed to have their friends for sleepovers in the caravan in the garden.

Emily had always loved the ruggedness of the North Cornish coast with its little coves and sandy bays. It had always been so quiet. She had encouraged the children to research places to go to whilst they were away.

Max wanted to go and see Boscastle, as the Scout group he went to had been caught in the floods there a few years ago and the photos were up in the Scout hall.

Emily planned to also take them up to Tintagel; she could remember feeling on top of the world when they had navigated all the steps to the top. And when they were back down in the village, they would always have a creamed tea, and Emily intended to extend this tradition to her own children.

Grace wanted to go and see the Cornish pixies. Emily had found a site on the Internet which gave a couple of possible places to go to.

Tania

Tania had known as she walked into the salon that her sister would be upset and waiting to get away; she had been quite emphatic that she wanted to leave before the rush hour and to get to Cornwall before it got late. But Tania also knew that she could not face a week in the dreary New Forest—all that open space, wild horses, cows, donkeys, and pigs and not a decent shopping centre in sight—without having her nails and hair done first. Last time she had visited, she had stayed in a five star hotel with a spa about a twenty-minute drive away; she had been able to have a manicure, massage, and pedicure after she had visited Emily and her father. God, she remembered that dreadful day when Emily had wanted to spend bonding time with her and had driven her to a local shopping centre just outside of Bournemouth and enthused about the different shops. Tania had found them all so boring. Did people still really shop in Next and Marks and Spencer's and get excited about it? Well, Emily certainly did and had got excited; even the coffee shops had been Costa and Nero.

Tania loved her life; she would not describe herself as rich—such a common term—but they were upper middle class and wealthy. James was able to always clear her credit card each month and ensure that the children went to a decent school where they boarded from Monday to Friday. James booked luxury breaks and holidays, and they both always had a new car each year. Tania was able to have a lady in to clean three times a week and a gardener/handyman came in twice a week. When the children were babies and toddlers before they went to prep school, Tania had a series of live-in au pairs who had looked after the children and their needs.

Tania always looked immaculate, as did her house and children. When they held one of their frequent dinner parties, Tania did not spend hours sweating over a stove. No, the only time Tania sweated was when she worked out with her trainer at the gym three times a week. For dinner parties, Tania had an outside caterer come in to do everything; the only thing she had to do apart from go to the salon and get dresses was to prepare the menu and supervise the seating plan, theme, and colour. Tania's dinner parties were popular; friends would do anything to get an invite and always cooed over Tania's hospitality and talent. Little did they know! Tania did not feel guilty; it was a foreign emotion to her. Tania took all the praise whilst ensuring that no one could find out about her little secret; she used a discreet company based in Kent.

Tania had never liked her hometown; all through her secondary school years, she dreamed of moving to London with her friend 'Tasha'. They spent endless nights, when they should have been studying, painting their nails, studying fashion magazines, and planning their escape and future success. Tania hated working, but she did have a Saturday job in a small boutique; she would laugh at her sister who went out each morning and one night a week delivering papers. Tania knew there were other ways of getting money without even moving out of the house; both their parents were too trusting. When they were in the last year of school, Tasha's dad suddenly got a promotion at the bank and had to transfer to London. Her parents decided that they would move the family near Greenwich so that her dad didn't have to spend hours away from his family commuting each day.

At sixteen, unbeknown to her parents, Tania applied for and was accepted at the same sixth form college that Tasha was going to. Tasha's parents agreed that Tania could stay with them week nights but would go home at weekends. This soon became term time only as both Tania and Tasha always had so much to do at weekends. This was the time that Tania met James; he was a colleague of Tasha's father and was six years older and already a successful name in the banking world. Two years later, Tania was pregnant; she dropped out of college and she and James got married.

Tania remembered the stress of planning her wedding. It had to be perfect; she had known exactly what she wanted, and Tania did not do compromise. Her mother was always trying to cut corners, but Tania was having none of it, and unlike her sister who had a registry office wedding and a garden party, she had had a very classy do. 'Mind you,' Tania thought, 'it was just as well our parents hadn't wasted money on a more lavish do for Emily, as Emily and Howard's marriage had only lasted a couple of years, so it would have been a waste of money.' Tania was smug. She knew people thought her own marriage would not last; she had even overheard some cow at the reception say that 'she had only married James for his money', but it was fourteen years ago and she was still happy. Who wouldn't be happy with a husband who could keep her in a better lifestyle year after year? Look at today, Tristan her hairdresser for the last year didn't come cheap. He was very selective as to which clients he did personally, and you paid for the privilege. She had had to wait for nearly two years to become a client; waiting was not something that Tania did, and now she did not want to lose him. Tania came in at least twice a week. Maybe, she mused, she could leave her father for a few hours and pop back for a day midweek. Emily would never know!

Tania relaxed back into the basin as a young girl—she could never remember her name—started to wash her hair and massage her scalp. Tania had a habit of being dismissive to anyone she considered to be beneath her, and Tania had no intention of having a conversation with her. She guessed that Emily would probably chat nineteen to the dozen, but then again, Emily rarely went to the hairdressers, and when she did she only went to the local salon.

Tania once more let her mind wander back to her wedding day. Tania had stamped her feet and cried and cajoled her parents, who eventually gave in and agreed to a five star country house hotel for the wedding and the reception. The hotel was very prestigious and near the coast; friends mainly from London all came down for the weekend and stayed at the hotel. Three of her friends, including Tasha, were bridesmaids; her mother had wanted her to have two younger children of cousins, but Tania put a ban on any children being present. The champagne flowed from breakfast time until James and herself were whisked off to the Maldives for a two-week honeymoon.

Tania suddenly realised that Tristan was speaking to her; she quickly clicked into 'flirt' mode and glided across the salon to sit before the master. Tristan could work miracles with Tania's hair; it always looked perfect, never had a visible regrowth, so everyone thought her hair was completely natural blonde.

Tania thought about her sister's hair—mousey brown and boring, normally pulled back into a ponytail. Tania could never wear her hair in a ponytail. Tania considered Emily boring; she had a boring life, lived in a boring town, and had a boring job. Emily had never been further than Northern France, once when she went with Howard camping; the thought of camping made Tania shudder, and Tristan asked if she was cold.

Tania would think about her family as little as possible and since her mother had died even less. Her mother had always insisted on phoning her once a week. Tania had found her parents useful; she despised the fact that the one point that James would not give on was the boys becoming full-time boarders. The fact that they came home on a Friday night and went back on a Monday morning and had half term and holidays cramped Tania's style. Often, Tania would drive down to the Forest on a Friday, drop the boys off with her parents, and jet off to Dublin or Paris with friends; it would be left to James to pick them up Sunday night, ready for school on the Monday. She was none too pleased that her sister had basically insisted that she go down so that she could have a break. It had been pure blackmail. Emily had bumped into Tasha's parents when they were in Bournemouth seeing family, and Emily had told them that she was 'so pleased that Tania was going to come down'. The parents had told Tasha. Tasha told her what an angel she was in front of their friends over lunch, and they all proclaimed that Tania was a hero. She was going to be slumming it and being a nursemaid, and was there no end to her talents? So Tania knew that she had to go down to maintain her face in front of her friends.

Hair done, Tania picked up the children from a friend's house and collected their packed cases from their hallway. James was coming down the next day and would be there until Tuesday. Once on to the M3, Tania cursed as she realised that she was going to get caught in the Friday traffic. Tania hated the drive down the M3, then the M27, and then the A31; the nearer she got, the more down she always felt. She could never think of this as going home; home was in London. As a teenager, she had never felt part of the 'scene'; she would rebel and used to go off into Bournemouth or Southampton to nightclubs from the time she was about fourteen years old. She would swear to her parents that she was at Tasha's and Tasha would swear she was at Tania's. When she did get caught out, she nearly always managed to wheedle her way out of trouble. Tania hated her sister's house. She hated the fact it was on an estate and attached; at least it wasn't a council house!

Tania wished Emily would agree to sell her parents' house and put their father into a home, then she would not be making this journey. Emily was stubborn; she had tried to explain to Tania that until she couldn't cope any longer she owed it to their mother to look after their father. Tania couldn't understand this—just because her mother and father had helped Emily! Their mother was dead; you couldn't owe a dead person something! Tania always referred to their parents as Mother and Father, never Mum and Dad. She insisted her own children called her Mummy and that they called James Daddy. Their parents, she thought, had plenty of money, good pensions, and investments; they never spent much or had loans or credit cards. Tania was so up herself that she had never questioned whether her parents could actually afford her lavish wedding. Only Emily knew the truth, hence her own discreet wedding.

Tania realised that as soon as she got on to the M27 the traffic was slowing down; she was only doing forty miles an hour in the fast lane. It would normally take only about half an hour from here. Tania realised that she was going to be even later and her sister would not be pleased. Eventually, when Tania turned on to her sister's drive she was just over two hours late.

Tania hooted her horn; she waited until her sister came to the door so that her car gave ultimate impact parked as it was next to Emily's little Clio. Tania glided out of the car. Straight away, Emily made a jealous remark about bank bonuses or banks being in trouble, but Tania knew her sister was always jealous of what she had, so she ignored her and pretended to be pleased to see her sister. She air-kissed her and apologised for being late, blaming the traffic.

Tania was taken straight through to the kitchen with Emily talking nineteen to dozen, issuing instructions and explanations. Tania suddenly started to pay attention when her sister said that their father was getting forgetful. Tania felt herself go pale, and panic started to rise up from her stomach. Was her sister implying that their father needed some physical care? But before Tania could collect herself and run back to London, Emily and her two children were out of the door and off.

Tania slowly turned and walked back into the house, closing the front door just as a dog appeared and placed his dirty paws on her trousers. 'Oh my God, she hasn't put the dog in kennels. Shoo, shoo,' she said, flapping her hands to push the dog towards the garden. Emily had not mentioned looking after the dog! Well, Tania was not going to have that responsibility, and she would soon let Emily know. 'Grant,' Tania shrieked for her son.

The Journey

Waving out of the window and feeling slightly guilty, Emily reversed out of her drive and they were off.

Emily prayed that they wouldn't get too caught up with traffic around the Ferndown bypass, which was notorious for snarl-ups especially on a Friday night and the start of the May half-term holidays.

As she had predicted, the nearer they got to Ferndown in Dorset, the more the traffic started to slow down. Roadworks for the Olympic games next year had been creating havoc for a while. Emily knew from experience that it would be slow going until she got to the other side of Bridport.

Silently, she cursed her sister, then smiled as she realised that her sister had no real idea of what she was actually letting herself in for. Emily was not a malicious person, but there were times when her sister needed to be brought down a peg or two. And maybe this holiday was one of those times. Emily knew that this was a one-off; there was no way that she would sit with her father again.

Tania was not the sort of sister that you could ring up and have a good moan to; Tania would always turn a conversation round to what she was doing—having fitted or a recent purchase or holiday.

Emily knew that her sister would have a rude awakening this week; she only hoped that she would not bother Wendy too much.

Max tuned the radio into Capital radio, and they all started to relax.

'Mummy, do you think Granddad will be OK with Auntie Tania and the boys?' asked Grace from the back seat.

'Of course, he will. Auntie Tania is his daughter. Isn't she like I am?' Emily tried to sound reassuring, trying to put more conviction into her voice than she actually felt. Was this all a bad idea? Would her dad be OK?

Grace pondered this for a few minutes like any nine-year-old would. 'But Auntie Tania doesn't like getting dirty, and if Granddad digs up the garden again she might get her trousers dirty, then get cross. Then Granddad will be upset.'

Guilt descended on to Emily's shoulders. Grace was right; her sister was not a carer. She liked to be cared for, but did not understand the first thing about looking after their dad. When her own boys were small, she always had an au pair to help out. Emily remembered the number of holidays when her nephews had been dumped on her parents. Her parents never minded and loved having all the children around them, but Emily knew that both boys always felt that they had been abandoned by their parents. Also, in Emily's house, she did not have all the mod cons that Tania had in her house and certainly not a cleaner or a dishwasher.

Emily had worked herself into a frenzy the weekend before, making sure that her house was clean, but with the dog, Dad, and the two children, it didn't stay clean for long.

Suddenly Emily remembered she had not told Tania when to feed Bruno, their very bouncy golden retriever, or when he liked to be walked or where to walk him; in fact, she couldn't remember even mentioning him to her. 'Oh, dear.'

Pushing the guilt aside, she decided that she would ring Wendy herself later when she got to Port Isaac and ask her to pop round the next day and check that everything was running OK and maybe ask her if she and her boys would offer to take Bruno out for a walk.

Then again, she felt guilty as she remembered that she had only just hoped that Tania would not bother Wendy and here she was already planning to ring her later. But at least Wendy was her friend. Wendy did not particularly like Tania, and Tania certainly looked down her nose at Wendy.

Life was so much of a juggling game—having more than three balls in the air most of the time and trying not to drop them.

This was another reason she had decided to enlist the reluctant help of her sister; she needed some quality time with her own children. Their own father never bothered to take them out or away.

The last time he had put in an appearance he had taken them to the local McDonalds, and they had returned after only two hours because his new wife—she could never think of either of them by name—had phoned to say that they were going out at six o'clock rather than seven, so he was needed home earlier. Neither of the children ever seemed outwardly that bothered at the lack of a father figure, and maybe having their granddad around made up for it a bit; they had spent a lot of time with their grandparents, and when he was first diagnosed and was in a lucid phase, he frolicked around with them as though he was a child, but unfortunately those phases had become less recently.

Emily looked in the rear-view mirror, and as she had predicted, Grace was fast asleep. She should stay asleep for most of the journey (which at this rate would take all night); she would be in a good mood once they got there.

It was now six fifteen, and the holiday traffic was well and truly underway. They had not got that far and already had been on the road for nearly an hour.

'Oh well,' thought Emily. 'There is nothing I can do about it, so I am going to relax and enjoy it.' Emily suggested to Max that they put on their 'travel' CD; this way they could sing along and stay alert.

Emily had always enjoyed the journey to Cornwall; as a child, she had always loved coming down the hill into Honiton and going past what looked like an old gatehouse, in which she had always been convinced a princess lived—maybe because it was painted pink.

That night as she came down the hill, Emily was disappointed to see that it was no longer pink but a more bland colour. She hoped her other memories would not be too shattered. The last time they had been in Cornwall was five years ago with both her mum and dad in the caravan. Emily had had to drive as her dad was already deteriorating. Emily had never towed the caravan before, but she had seized the task like she always did and decided, 'Either I drive or we don't go.' Emily and the children had slept in the awning. Her mum had asked her to sell the caravan and car when she realised that her husband would not be able to drive any more. She had felt that it would put any temptation out of harm's way.

Although Emily knew that she had to go right at the roundabout, then left on to the dual carriageway to get to Exeter, she recovered from her disappointment over the pink house and involved Max in telling her the route from his meticulous plans.

'At the roundabout, we need to turn right,' Max said as though reading her thoughts. 'Then we need to turn left.'

Four hours after setting off, Emily found herself navigating the small streets around Port Isaac two hours late.

She decided to leave the car at the top of the harbour and walk down to the pub, as she thought she could phone Gwen on the way down.

Emily woke Grace, and together the three of them set off for the harbour, looking over the harbour wall down into the main harbour itself; it seemed very busy. Although it was nearly nine thirty, there seemed lots of people around, and Emily presumed they could all be enjoying the mild evening and were either eating or drinking out or returning from walking over the coastal route.

Gwen answered on the second ring and arranged to meet them in ten minutes. All three of them were hungry and thirsty;

Emily decided that as it was their first night they would have a meal in the bar before going to the cottage.

As they drew nearer to the harbour, Emily realised that a film crew were filming and remembered that the programme *Doc Martin* was filmed in and around the area with the doctor's surgery based in the village.

The children were fascinated by all the Hubbub, people running around shouting and calling for silence.

Emily held the children back as a man put his arm out to prevent them from going any further; he turned and gave Emily an apologetic look. Emily smiled back with what she hoped was a reassuring look that would explain that she didn't mind and that she quite understood.

Once the camera started to roll, the harbour took on a deathly quiet air; one man stood at the bottom by the waves, looking at another man who was lying in the water. 'He's dead,' he said and marched up the hill.

Emily realised that it was the actor Martin Clunes, the main character; he played the gruff doctor who did not have any bedside manner and could always be relied upon to be rude to his patients. She looked around and saw other characters that she recognised from the little she had seen of the programme.

Well, this would be something to talk about once they got home, and they hadn't even made it into the cottage yet.

As she thought about home, she remembered that she needed to ring Wendy about the dog, but here Emily felt free and not at all intimidated by her sister, so she decided to text Tania: 'Hi forgot to say Bruno's food under the sink, one tin and biscuits morning and night and he needs at least two walks a day, usually stay out about twenty minutes xx. ps. Arrived safe!'

She pressed send, then waited for the icon to say it had gone; pressing off, she closed her phone. Then she slipped it into her handbag, feeling guilty.

Once the man allowed them to pass with a wink in Emily's direction, Emily took the children each by the hand and guided them into the pub which was situated next to the slipway.

'Cor, Mum, look,' said Max, 'that sign says live crabs.'

Emily looked across the slipway to the sign.

'Yes, love, that's what people do. They buy the live crabs, then cook them for salads and sandwiches.'

Max looked at her in disbelief.

Emily decided that unless she wanted to get involved in a conversation with her son that she might not know all the answers to, then she needed to distract him quickly.

'Right, who's for a coke?'

Both children replied, 'Please.' This was a treat; Emily tried to ensure that they all ate and drank healthy foods.

Emily found them a table and went to the bar to collect the three cokes and a menu.

A middle-aged lady in a summer floral dress came up to Emily and introduced herself, 'You must be Emily. I am Gwen.'

Both women shook hands.

Emily instantly liked her; she seemed the homely type, reminding Emily of her own mother.

Gwen joined them at the table.

'If you're looking for something to eat, I would recommend the sausage and mash. The chef does a mean mash potato and the sausages are local. The gravy is . . . to die for.' Both children giggled.

Gwen gave an apologetic grin. 'I think I spend too much time in here.'

Both children looked at Emily expectantly. 'Yes, please, Mum.'

Gwen indicated to the bar man. 'Four sausages and mash, George.' It proved that she did indeed spend too much time in the pub.

'Righto, Gwen, give us ten minutes,' George replied.

Turning to Emily, Gwen said, 'I hope you don't mind me joining you, but I have been to Truro today to visit my mother in the nursing home and I am so hungry.'

Emily and Gwen sat talking about their parents whilst they all ate the meal;

The children spent the time people watching.

Both women had similar problems with regard to looking after their parents, but Gwen's mother had been still of sound mind if not body when she decided that she would go into a nursing home rather than be a burden on Gwen, even if it meant that Gwen had to clock up the miles up and down the road to Truro every other day.

Emily was quick to reassure Gwen that her dad wasn't a burden and that she loved having him live with her; it added colour to their lives, and although the children found it difficult to understand their grandfather's behaviour from time to time, they were able to at least have him in their lives for a while longer.

Emily knew there would come a time when she would need to think about putting her cherished dad into a home and sell the house to help to pay for it, but it was still too soon, and she would not be beholden to her sister. Dad did have some money in the bank and it would pay for a few years of care, but Emily was having to use all his pension on the day care centre, so not much was being added to his bank account; unless the house was sold, the money wouldn't last. Emily knew her sister thought that their parents had money, but the truth was that even fourteen years ago, Tania's wedding had cost in excess of 20,000 pounds and their parents had struggled to find the money, cashing in insurance policies and savings bonds, hence, her own small wedding. Emily noticed that the children were starting to argue; this was usually an indicator that they were both tired.

Reaching for her purse, Emily got up to go and pay for the meals, noticing that Gwen made no attempt to offer to pay for her own meal. 'You paying for all four then?' said George.

'Yes, please,' replied Emily. George raised his eyebrow and gave her a smile that indicated that he wasn't surprised by this.

Back at the table, Emily asked the children to pick up their things so that they could make their way to the cottage.

Gwen walked back to the car with them. 'My van is over there. Follow me.' Gwen stopped by a rusty old Ford which had seen better days, Five minutes later, they pulled up outside a small fishing cottage. From the outside, it looked like all the others in the row—small windows, whitewashed walls, and a red front door; a closer inspection would soon show that the cottage needed a bit more than TLC.

Tania's First Night

As soon as Tania had gotten Grant to put the dog outside, she groaned. Emily's kitchen was antiquated; she saw a bottle of washing-up liquid and some Marigold gloves on the sink and panicked. 'I, Tania Louise Clifton-Peters, is expected to wash up, OMG!' There was *no* dishwasher; slowly, it dawned on Tania that washing-up meant cooking; cooking meant washing-up.

She could hear her two boys talking in the lounge and realised that they must be talking to their grandfather, and she had not even said hello to her father yet. 'Even though he won't recognise me,' she muttered as she walked into the lounge. 'Hi, Father.' Her father grunted; the room smelt of old people and pee.

Both boys looked at her, two pairs of large blue eyes, the same colour as her own. 'We are starving, Mummy. Please, can we have supper?' whined Adam. Tania groaned again; at home, she would be putting an upmarket ready meal into her microwave oven, along with a bag of washed leaves and tomatoes and other salad bits. Here she opened the fridge to find vegetables, potatoes, four chicken breasts, and a supermarket trifle plus a bottle of Pinot Grigio white wine. What was she meant to do with them? And the wine was undrinkable—so cheap; she was used to superior wine or champagne. They imported all the wine they drank at home; it was never bought from a supermarket. It would never cross Tania's mind that her sister had made a nice gesture by putting the wine in the fridge; grabbing her bag, she told the boys they were going to the local gastro pub.

Neither of the boys complained; as long as they got food at their age, it didn't matter where they ate. None of their friends' mums did much cooking except for Greg. His mum was a great cook; she made cakes, biscuits, pies, meals, and pizzas from scratch. All the boys at school loved to go there as they all knew they would get a warm welcome and a brilliant tea. Grant had stayed overnight a few weekends ago and had been given a cooked breakfast on the Sunday morning, not muesli like he had to have at home but a full English breakfast like they had when they went away on holidays to their grandparents or the occasional breaks when their mother allowed them to accompany their parents.

As Tania ushered them both out through the front door, Grant asked, 'What about Grandfather?'

Tania suddenly realised she would need to take her father with them. 'No, wait.' Wasn't there a fish and chip shop round the corner? She could send the boys when they got back. She would just leave him watching TV; he hadn't moved since they had arrived, so he wouldn't be going anywhere.

Two and a half hours later, Tania started to realise the enormity of the task she had taken on; she had made her first mistake! As she pulled up into the drive, she saw that the front door was wide open. The boys jumped out and ran inside, checking every room, whilst Tania stood looking at the door. Tania was no good in a crisis. She never knew how to take control; she had been sheltered all her life, first by her parents and then by her husband.

'Hello there.' Tania turned and noticed an elderly woman waving at her. 'Oh no, bloody nosey neighbours' was her first thought.

'I think I might have what you are looking for sitting in my kitchen.' Tania looked at her. 'Mrs Greggs,' said the woman, offering a hand. Tania ignored the hand, whilst Mrs Greggs thought to herself, 'She is as stuck up as they said she was.' Mrs Greggs continued to explain with

some reproach in her voice that she had found her father wandering in
the road. 'Emily would never leave him. That's why she has asked you to
stay.'

Tania seethed; so Emily was the golden girl as far as Mrs Greggs
and probably all the neighbours were concerned. 'Saint bloody Emily,'
thought Tania as she swept past Mrs Greggs, who indicated where
her father was. Tania quickly got her father back into the house and
slammed the door before Mrs Greggs could follow. Adam noticed that
his grandfather had wet trousers; this was amusing for a ten-year-old
and he started to laugh. Grant was the more sensitive of the two boys,
who took after his father; he glared at Adam. Tania sent him to change;
ten minutes later, she found him sitting in front of the television still
in the same jogging bottoms. It was quickly now dawning on her that
Emily had lied to her; she had deliberately not told her how bad their
father was. It was obvious that he should be in a home, not here where
his daughter had to look after his intimate needs. How was she, Tania,
going to get him changed? The boys quickly assessing the situation
suggested they go to the fish and chip shop to get his tea. They decided
to take Bruno with them.

Left on her own, Tania felt that she was in a nightmare. How
did you change an old man? Eventually, Tania got her father into his
pyjamas and had just sat him down at the kitchen table when the boys
brought back the fish and chip supper. Second mistake—Tania realised
that she would need to help her father to eat as he sat staring at the
plate; she had never even fed her own children, and she had left the
messy side of things to the au pair. Tania fuming and cross almost
force-fed her father whilst the two boys started to argue; neither were
used to having no satellite television or no Wii or Game Boy. To defuse
the situation, Tania suggested that they phone their daddy and then go
for a shower.

By the time she had got both boys and her father into bed and taken
a shower herself, it was 11 p.m. There was no way she was going to
spend a week here. The shower was awful; it had no power. She looked

at her mobile phone and saw the message from her sister; no way—no way was that dog getting two twenty-minute walks a day. He could stay outside during the day unless the boys wanted to walk him. Still fuming, Tania turned off the light; the bed was uncomfortable, so were the pillows, and although she knew all the linen was clean, it was cheap and chafed her skin. The curtains were also thin, and Tania knew that as soon as it was first light she would be woken up. Another thought passed through her mind. 'What if he called out in the night, how will I cope?' Tania lay awake, tossing and turning. By midnight, Tania had decided that the next day she would phone Emily and demand that she returned home immediately, and if she refused, she would leave their father to the mercy of the local social services. No human being should have to live like this, looking after elderly relatives!

The Cottage

Gwen came round to the car door, holding up a set of keys.

'Follow me, folks.' Gwen marched up to the front door.

Emily noticed the garden was overgrown; the brochure had said a typical fishing cottage, but the picture had been of a tidy and well-stocked garden.

Gwen opened the front door which led straight into the lounge area. There was a musty smell. Everything looked a bit tired, but Emily decided that in the morning it would all look better; they needed to sleep.

Gwen pointed to a door. 'That's the stairs. Over there is the bathroom, and that's the kitchen.'

Gwen passed the keys to Emily.

'I live just up the street at number nine, so if you need anything just let me know. Any problems, and I will get George to sort them out.'

Emily wondered if this was the same George she had met earlier in the bar.

As Gwen shut the door, Emily turned round to the children.

'Right, it's nearly eleven o'clock, so let's quickly empty the car, dump everything in the lounge, and then go to bed' Emily was glad that Grace had spent the journey asleep, as she still had some spark in her, although Emily couldn't wait to get into bed herself.

It took three journeys for them to empty the car.

Max started to moan that if his sister hadn't brought so much they would have finished sooner. Emily made allowances and ignored him as she was aware that they were all tired. Luckily, they would all be able to have a nice lie-in; tomorrow would be a chill day.

Emily found the bag with the toiletries and nightwear; she had had the forethought to pack these separately just in case they were late.

'Right, up the stairs.' As she turned on the light to go up the stairs, all the lights went out.

'Mum,' cried Grace.

'It's OK. The brochure says that we need to put money in the meter. Let's wait until the morning and pretend we are camping tonight.'

Emily didn't like to admit she had no idea where the meter was and would need to search for it in the morning, but as she didn't have a torch and the street light did not give enough light to help her, she wasn't going to look tonight, nor did she know whether it took a card or coins.

Upstairs, the children each decided they wanted one of the back bedrooms as they would be able to see the harbour in the morning.

This left Emily with the small single bedroom at the front.

Too tired to argue, she allowed the children to each take a bedroom and went into her room; she could sort it all out in the morning.

'Mum, there aren't any sheets on the bed.' This was Max calling her.

Emily looked at her bed and what she could see in the light from the street lamp outside. A pile of linen sat on the bed, ready for the beds to be made up. Emily wished she had brought their own duvets. She quickly realised that she would need to make up all three beds before they would be able to go to sleep tonight. 'OK, coming.'

Emily woke up early the next morning and drew back her curtains; there was a light mist hanging around the chimney pots and heavy dew on the grass outside.

Emily turned round and looked at the room. It was no good; she would have to bargain with Grace and swap rooms. The bed was only a single bed and not really long enough for Emily's five foot eight frame; she had not got much sleep trying to get comfortable.

Quietly, Emily slipped down the stairs, not wanting to wake Grace up. Max would sleep though most things, but if Grace was up too early, she would end up grumpy later in the day.

Once in the kitchen, Emily realised that the cottage was certainly not all that it was advertised to be. It was dated; some might call it quaint, but Emily thought it was tired and in need of a good clean. Her own home wasn't ultra modern, not like her sister's, but it was a home. It was spotlessly clean. Emily spent evenings and weekends cleaning up after the two children, dog, and her dad. Emily hated grubby; she did wonder but dismissed it quickly how Tania was getting on. Dad would normally start shouting 'tea, tea' around six o'clock each morning.

Opening the fridge door, she remembered that the electric had run out the previous night.

'Right,' she muttered to herself. 'Where would the meter be?'

Opening the cupboard under the stairs, Emily saw the meter straight away and groaned. It was the type with new key card meters; they would need to find a shop to top it up.

Emily turned on the hot tap; luckily, within minutes it started to belch out hot water. The gas was obviously not on a meter, or if it was, it was still topped up.

Digging around in one of the boxes of essentials, Emily found her Marigold gloves and bottles of cleaning products; she would have the kitchen cleaned up before the children came down. Emily always packed a box of cleaning products ever since the children had been babies and they had gone to a certain national park and found the chalet filthy dirty, with ants crawling all over the surface. She had had to even clean the bath on that particular holiday before she could bathe the children. They had moved to another site the next day, which had cost them more money, but money wasn't everything; the children always came first where Emily was concerned.

Emily spent the next hour and a half cleaning all the kitchen surfaces—fridge, cupboards, cooker hob—and scrubbing the table. She decided, on opening the oven, that she was not going to start cleaning it; if necessary, they would eat out. She then found a mop and bucket in the cupboard and gave the floor a good clean. Emily stood back, looking satisfied; after her chat with Gwen the previous night, she wasn't surprised that the cottage seemed unloved.

Now she decided that the last job she would do was to wash the windows as she wasn't able to see out of them. Emily knew this was a silly thing to do to a house they were only renting for a week, but she liked to look out into a garden and would want to watch what the children were up to if they were outside. Plus, it gave her something to do; if she stopped, she knew she would start thinking about home. She would worry about her dad and how Tania was coping.

Taking a fresh bucket of water and a cloth, she opened the back door, emerging into a weedy patch of lawn with a jungle or a natural wilderness of a garden at the bottom, depending on how you looked at it. She could see daffodils poking through the long grass. Well, maybe there was a mower in the shed or she could ask Gwen if George could come and cut the lawn so that they could use the garden. Emily found a rather unsafe-looking chair to reach the windows.

Looking up, she noticed that the sun was starting to peep through the mist and the day looked promising. Emily had already decided that they would stay close to the cottage today and investigate the village.

It was still only eight thirty, and Emily guessed that the shops wouldn't be open yet, but she really did want a cup of coffee.

Suddenly, Emily heard a voice over the fence.

'Hi, I see Gwen has managed to get a guest to live in there then.'

Peering over the fence, Emily saw an elderly white-haired lady with a warm, friendly face.

'Hello,' Emily smiled down at the lady; holding out her hand, she introduced herself.

'Mary,' said the elderly lady. 'I bet you would love a cup of coffee or tea, my dear.'

Emily smiled at Mary, 'I was just wondering where I could go to get the meter topped up.'

Mary smiled and shook her head.

'Just like Gwen not to leave any electric on the card. The shop is only five minutes' walk down the hill, but it doesn't open till nine o'clock. I see you have children. I saw a young boy and a little girl when you came in last night.'

Mary suggested that Emily should wait and she would bring them both out a cuppa.

Emily found two chairs that looked as if they would hold their weight and moved the table closer to the pathway.

Going inside, she brought out a cloth and cleaner to give the table a wipe, just as Mary appeared with two cups of hot fresh coffee and a plate of Danish pastries.

Emily suddenly realised that her cleaning spree and the smell of the Danishes had made her really hungry, and she sank down on to one of the chairs gratefully.

Emily invited Mary to sit down.

Emily looked at Mary as she gratefully sank her teeth into an apricot Danish. 'Um, delicious. Have you lived here long?'

Mary started to explain how she had lived in the village for seventy-three years, having been born in London and bred in Cornwall, and that she had also raised her own family in the same house.

Mary had known Gwen for the last forty or more years; it was obvious that Mary liked a good old gossip. Gwen had apparently bought the cottage when she had lost her husband and then shortly after that the second cottage, and now she used this cottage as an income. 'Not much income though.' Mary told Emily that she wasn't sure how Gwen's husband had died, but she knew it had been an accident and that there were no children from the marriage.

Mary explained that Gwen tended not to do much to the cottage, and most clients that came and stayed had been doing so for a number of years and were regulars. Most used it just as a base for the walking they did around the area. Mary explained that there were good opportunities for walking; there was the coastal path or there were inland walks, and also, lots of people used the Camel trail. Mary saw that Emily looked bemused, and she explained that the Camel trail ran from Bodmin to Padstow through Wadebridge, and you could either walk on it or ride bikes which could be hired as the trail was car free. Emily liked the sound of a bike ride.

Emily looked up when she heard a noise in the kitchen; a very sleepy Grace appeared at the door.

Emily introduced her daughter and the older lady to each other. Grace snuggled up on to her mum's knee and accepted the last half of the Danish pastry that was on her mum's plate.

Mary stood up to take her leave. 'You know, I miss my grandchildren. They live in North Yorkshire, and I only see them a couple of times a year. If you want to go out, my dear, I would be happy to come round and sit with the children.'

Emily thanked her for her kindness, not only for the offer of babysitting but also for the coffee and pastries, explaining that she didn't actually know anyone in the area to go out with.

When Mary left, Emily decided that if they didn't drag Max out of bed, then he would be there forever.

Grace and Emily both went back upstairs, Emily carrying some of her daughter's bags and Grace carrying the rest.

'Sorry, love, but we are going to have to swap rooms. Mummy cannot stretch out in this small bed.' Emily gave Grace an apologetic smile.

To her surprise, Grace agreed straight away, and Emily gave her daughter a big hug and a kiss. 'Thank you, darling.'

Max was not so happy to be woken up, but he agreed to get dressed and start sorting out his belongings and lay the breakfast table whilst

Emily and Grace went into the village in search of electric, milk, and some hot pasties, Mary having told them that there was a genuine Cornish pasty shop by the harbour that sold not only traditional meat pasties but also sweet pasties.

Max was a growing lad and the way to his heart was definitely through his stomach, and the promise of fresh Cornish pasties for breakfast immediately grabbed his interest.

Tania First Morning

Tania woke up from what felt like a deep fog. 'What was that noise?' She could hear 'tea, tea'. Looking at the clock, she saw that it was only six fifteen in the morning. Tania realised she had only had about five hours' proper sleep, and she needed eight; if she didn't, then her hair and skin suffered, and if they suffered so did everyone else around her. She had tossed and turned all night in the uncomfortable bed; she missed her pure Egyptian cotton sheets. The mattress had been rock hard, the pillows fibre filled, and the curtains had let in light since around a quarter to five, now this noise. If it was the boys playing up, they would both be in serious trouble.

Pulling on her pale blue silk negligee over her pale blue satin pyjamas and putting her feet into her mules, Tania ventured out on to the landing. The noise was coming from her father's room; gingerly she opened the door. The smell hit her; it was obvious that he had wet himself and the bed, but he was sitting up in bed, repeating the words 'tea, tea'.

'Father,' Tania almost shouted at him, 'it's barely six o'clock. What the hell do you think you're doing?' Tania was seriously annoyed; she never rose at this time of the morning and did not intend to do so for a whole week!

'Tea, tea.'

'Oh, be quiet, you stupid old man.' Tania stormed out of the room, banging the door shut; she did not for one moment stop to consider the boys sleeping across the small landing.

Tania headed straight for the bathroom; it was so uncivilised to have to share a bathroom. At home, Tania had an en suite and James used the guest bathroom next door unless they had guests, and then he would have to fit in with her own bathroom routine before he could use the room himself. The boys used the main bathroom when they were home, and Tania was thinking about having internal shower rooms installed in each of their rooms before the summer so that they did not argue about whose turn it was to go first in the morning and wake her up.

Back out on the landing, Tania could hear Grant speaking to his grandfather, 'Would you like a cup of tea? Is that what you need?' Tania thought it must be because her father was acting like a child that Grant could understand him; she would never give credit that Grant was just a sensitive kid who could tune into others' emotions and consider their needs.

'Mum.' Grant turned round as his mother came out of the bathroom. 'Grandfather would like a cup of tea. Shall I go down and make you both one?'

Tania glared at her son. 'Heaven forbid! Do I look like a woman who drinks tea at this hour of the morning?' Slamming the door, Tania retreated into the bedroom.

Grant and Adam were both self-sufficient boys; they had to be. They had learnt early on that if they needed anything, then it did no good to ask their mother. If the au pair was not around or they were between girls, usually because their mother had shouted and roared at them for no real reason, then the boys made their own breakfast and sometimes lunch in the holidays and had to entertain themselves if their father was not around.

Grant decided that maybe it would be best to just keep out of his mother's way this morning and try to keep his grandfather quiet. He returned his head round the door. 'OK, Grandfather, I will make the tea.' He noticed a small television in the corner of the room and decided that this might keep him occupied whilst he was downstairs. Adam was still asleep, so he left his door shut so he was not disturbed.

Ten minutes later, the dog was in the garden. Grant had replenished his water bowl and put a tin of food—presuming that Bruno was a large dog. Reading the label, the can said one tin and biscuits; everything was under the sink. Leaving the back door open and shutting the hall door securely so the dog did not follow him through and upstairs, Grant carried a tray of tea and toast upstairs for himself and his grandfather. He placed the tray on the small table and opened the curtains and the window. It was a bit smelly in the room, but then didn't all old people smell? According to his mates at school, their grandparents smelt old and musty. Grant settled down to help his grandfather to eat his toast and drink his tea.

Grant sat with his grandfather watching the television until he heard the dog barking and the doorbell ringing at eight o'clock. Going downstairs, knowing that his mother would not reappear, Grant opened the door to find a care worker on the steps.

'Hello, you must be Adam or Grant. Your auntie told me you would be staying. My name is Marie. Your mum should be expecting me to help get your granddad up.'

Grant looked blank.

'Auntie Emily left a long list of instructions on the door for your mum in the kitchen. Where is she?' Marie looked slightly worried.

Grant knew he shouldn't let people into the house, but all things pointed to her being OK. Opening the door a little wider, Marie was able to enter the hallway.

'OK, where is your mum?'

Grant looked embarrassed. 'In bed.'

Marie looked at Grant. 'Do you think you could wake her, love? I only have three-quarters of an hour to get your granddad up, bathed, and dressed before my next client and I need her help.'

Grant looked worried now; both he and Adam knew that they only woke their mother if the house was burning down. Hopping uncomfortably from one foot to the other, he told Marie, 'We aren't allowed into Mother's room for any reason, none at all.'

Marie had been warned by Emily that Tania was lazy, so taking matters into her own hands, she marched upstairs and knocked on the bedroom door.

'Tania, it's Marie, your dad's carer.' Nothing.

She banged a bit louder. The door burst open.

'What the bloody hell is going on? Who let you in?'

Marie sidestepped the last question and extended her hand. 'Nice to meet you.' She started to explain who she was and why she needed help.

Tania looked appalled. 'You want me to help you? You are expecting me to help you? Who do you think pays for you to attend to my father? And you expect help?' Tania was livid; she was accentuating each word with a point of her finger.

Standard procedures for personal safety told Marie that she needed to leave, but her loyalty was torn; she really liked Emily and her immediate family. She knew the strain Emily had been under lately looking after her dad, the children, house, and garden and working at the school. She was aware of how much Emily needed this break, and if she walked away now, she was sure that this madam in front of her would be on the telephone demanding that Emily came home the minute she left the house.

At that moment, Grant reappeared. 'It's OK. I will help with Grandfather.' Tania turned on her heels and slammed the bedroom door once again, this time succeeding in waking up Adam.

Grant suggested Adam go and watch television and get himself some cereal and juice whilst he turned to Marie, who he predicted did not think he would be capable of helping her.

Marie was concerned; whilst she had worked with young carers before who helped to look after their parents, she had never been in this situation before. But she needed to get on, and she knew that the grandfather needed to be gotten out of bed.

Together, they worked to get his grandfather out of bed and into the shower and then dressed; they worked well together. Marie had a sense of humour and tried to keep things light as a way of making Grant more comfortable with the situation.

Whilst Grant was putting on his grandfather's socks and shoes, Marie stripped and changed the bed, knowing that Tania wouldn't do so. She noted that if Tania had put incontinence pants on her father the night before, then this would not be needed to be done.

Marie knew that Emily only had help once a day so she could get herself and the children to school on time, but she wondered 'could she manage to come back later and help to get Mr P into bed ?'she could see otherwise that maybe it would be left to Grant.

Marie and Grant helped his grandfather into his chair. Marie was impressed by the way that Grant talked and managed his grandfather.

Marie took Grant through into the kitchen, put the sheets into the wash, and showed Grant the list. She went through it with him, explaining anything that might cause him confusion. She was worried about putting the responsibility for his medication on to such a young teenager, but Emily had already put the tablets in a special box, which covered morning and night each day. Marie noticed that his night tablets for the day before hadn't been given to him last evening. Well, at least they were not for controlling any life-threatening illnesses. She removed these from the box and made a lengthy note in the day care book before saying goodbye to both boys and their grandfather.

It was gone ten in the morning when Tania finally appeared downstairs, looking bleary-eyed.

Grant started to explain to his mother what the care worker had told him, including the need to use the incontinence pants at night to save the bed. Grant continued to tell her that Marie had put the washing machine on, but they would need to put the clothes on the line to dry.

All Tania could reply was 'So she bloody should. She is being paid.' Tania never curbed her language in front of the boys, although it never normally got much worse than it was at present and would mostly only be directed at their father or one of the hired help.

Both Adam and Grant knew that the only way to avoid one of their mother's tempers was to disappear, this at home would be to the summer house where they had all their electronic gadgets to play on. Today, Grant decided that taking Bruno for a walk would be the best escape, dragging Adam with him.

As they left with an excited Bruno, a lady appeared at the back door. 'Hi, Tania.' The boys disappeared; their mother obviously knew her. 'Remember me? Wendy.'

Tania looked at her, her normal look of contempt on her face. Scowling, she threw at her, 'What do you want?'

'Just thought I'd pop in, see if you wanted anything.'

'No, we don't and I don't do popping in. Goodbye.' With that, Tania turned on her kitten heels and marched out of the kitchen.

Wendy stood completely amazed. 'The cow! She was so rude.' Well, Emily had warned her. Wendy thought it best to check up for Emily that her dad was actually OK. She found him sitting in his chair with the television on mute; with a sigh, she said hello and turned up the television so he could hear it. Wendy was used to the routine that Emily had her dad in and knew it was past coffee time; she knew Emily's kitchen well and set about making them both coffee and biscuits, which she carried into the lounge. 'Hi, Mr Peters, how are you today?'

'We are fine. What are you doing? How dare you interfere?' Tania stood in the doorway, seething.

Wendy turned calmly. 'It's gone his snack and coffee time, and he needs routine so I made the coffee.'

Tania moved quickly and removed the tray. 'You silly fool, if he drinks he wets. If he wets, who will change him?'

Wendy was concerned. 'You cannot stop him drinking. He will become ill. Old people need fluids.'

'I will decide what my father needs. Now leave this house.'

Wendy left before the situation deteriorated any further with a casual 'You have my number'.

Tania gathered up the half drunk cup and poured it down the sink. She rang James.

'Hi, honey, how's it going?'

'It isn't.' Tania sounded like a petulant child, but James could handle her most of the time just by agreeing rather than arguing. 'I can't do this. He needs proper care, not Saint Emily.' Tania continued to fill James in on her version of events.

'Sweetheart, you should *not* be doing this,' soothed James. 'Can't we put him into a hospital or an old people's home?'

Tania and James continued to moan about Emily and how inconsiderate she was for a further ten minutes until the boys reappeared and wanted to talk to their father.

'Be there in about an hour, honey, and we will sort something out.'

After the boys had said goodbye to their father, they went through to say hello to their grandfather. Adam wandered back through to the kitchen and helped himself to an apple from the bowl of fruit Emily had left for them. 'Grandfather is wet again.' He held his fingers to his nose, indicating a smell.

'That's it. We are going home,' Tania said firmly. Adam who was the same ilk as his mother was pleased; he hated being stuck in this house with nothing to do, and he wasn't keen on spending time with his grandfather now that he was an 'old' man.

Tania grabbed her mobile and dialled her sister's number, but the mobile went straight to voicemail. 'This is Emily. Please leave a message and I will get back to you.'

Tania shouted into the phone. 'Emily, Emily, where the hell are you? I can't cope.'

Tania threw the phone on the table. 'The bitch! She knew this would happen.'

Tania dialled again and again and left the same message that she had done before, but each time the phone went to voicemail. Eventually extremely angry, she texted: 'You bitch, you selfish cow, how could you do this to me?'

Tania stormed into the kitchen and started opening cupboard doors and slamming them shut; she searched under the stairs and finally in the lounge until she found what she was looking for. It took twenty-three phone calls before she succeeded in her mission; finally she rang a taxi.

As James pulled on to the drive, she ran out to greet him.

'Darling, how are you?' James took her into his embrace as she burst into tears.

'It's sorted out. I have a taxi on its way. I have paid for a month in advance.'

'Woo, start again.' James continued to soothe her hair.

'I have found my father a home where he should be! Oh, here's the taxi.'

James slightly bemused by the flood of events followed Tania back inside. 'Hi, Dad.' No response.

'You see, completely senile.' Tania started to haul her father out of the chair. Grant came to her assistance, gently cajoling his grandfather.

Tania gave the driver the name and address in Bournemouth of the care home and a small bag.

Mrs Greggs came out to see what was happening whilst Tania bundled her father into the waiting taxi.

Ten minutes later, with the promise from James of an overnight stay in a five star county house near Brockenhurst, Tania slammed her sister's front door and pushed the keys back through the letter box and climbed into her car.

Mrs Greggs, who by this time had called Wendy, stood together on Mrs Gregg's driveway.

'Well, I never did,' muttered Mrs Greggs.

'Oh, I can believe it.' Wendy was furious. 'She is a selfish madam. Bet she hadn't even given Bruno a thought.'

Wendy marched home to collect the spare set of keys she had for Emily's house. Letting herself in, she was met by a frantic Bruno; she let him straight out into the back garden. Wendy looked round. The place was a mess; nothing had been put away, and Wendy became angrier as she put her head around every room. She was glad her husband had taken the children out to the park; she texted him, telling him they would be having a guest, but it would be four legged not two, and then she set about tidying up. Wet towels were on the bathroom floor, beds unmade, curtains still drawn. Wendy stripped the beds, ready for Emily to make up when she came home and put the windows on vent. She scooped up the towels and went down to the kitchen. There was a pile of washing-up in the sink, and Wendy noticed that there were wet sheets in the washing machine. Oh, well, she knew that if she had been in the same situation Emily would do the same for her, so she set to doing the washing-up and putting it away and dragging out the washing and hanging it on the line. Returning to the kitchen, she noticed Mr Peters' medication on the table. She decided to give Marie a ring and quickly wrote down her number before putting on the other sheets to wash; she would pop back later. Calling Bruno, she picked up the bag with his food and bowls and went home.

Grant

Grant sat looking out of the car window, listening to his iPod. Unlike his mother, Grant actually enjoyed the journey down to the New Forest; he associated this journey with freedom and fun. Grant knew that his brother wasn't that bothered whether he did or didn't visit and would often moan whenever they had stayed with their grandparents that he was bored. Grant never found it boring; he had what his grandfather had called an 'old head on young shoulders'. Grant didn't really understand what this meant, but he knew that his grandfather was paying him a compliment, which was not something that often happened to Grant. Grant knew he would never be as clever as Adam. Adam was a straight A student. Grant hated school; his reports always said things like 'could try harder', 'lacks concentration'. Grant hated the uniform. Who at thirteen years old still had to wear shorts? At his school, the boys didn't wear long trousers till their senior year. Grant had been a weekly boarder since he was four years old. He had missed home when he had first gone away to school home and even now loved Fridays when he knew he would be going home for the weekend. Most Fridays, his dad managed to collect him and Adam, but if he was working then his mother would quite often collect them and bring them down to spend the weekend with their grandparents.

Grant struggled to understand instructions, especially when they were given at speed; words didn't make a lot of sense either. His grandfather had always understood. Grant could still clearly remember the fuss his mother had made when his grandfather tried to explain to her that he thought Grant was dyslexic. Grant had managed to look the word up on the Internet and it made sense with regard to most of the signs and symptoms he suffered, but his mother would have none of it. She shouted that there was nothing abnormal about either of her sons; she had turned and glared at Grant and called him 'bloody lazy'. His grandmother had tried to soothe things over by gently explaining that Grant could be helped, but this had made the situation worse, and his mother had dragged him and Adam back to London. Grant was not sure how they had gotten there in one piece; his mother had been in such a rage.

That had been the last time they had spent a holiday in the New Forest, and when his grandmother had become ill, Grant had been convinced that it was somehow his fault. One Saturday, his father had taken him out and explained to him exactly what was wrong with her and how it was nothing to do with him.

Grant was good at sports and loved the outdoors, which was why he loved the New Forest; he also enjoyed science. Grant was sensitive. He hated his mother's attitude to people, especially the way she treated his father's family whom he loved. They were such normal people; they led normal lives and did family things. Grant noticed that his auntie and uncle always included his cousins in everything they did. They went to their local schools. This disgusted his mother; she called them 'provincial'. Grant wasn't sure if it was meant for the school or his cousins, but he thought it was probably both. Grant wasn't sure what provincial meant, but by the tone of his mother's voice he knew it wasn't nice.

Grant sat up straight as his mother started to curse the traffic; they were now on the A31, and this was always slow at this time of the evening. It happened every time, in Grant's opinion, which he didn't dare voice. It was his mother's own fault; she hadn't needed to go and have her hair done. She had deliberately booked her appointment at the same time that she had told Auntie Emily that they would leave. Grant had heard her on the phone that morning; his school had broken up on the Thursday before and they had two weeks off. His mother had told the salon that 'my sister will just have to wait'. So surely his mother could work out they would bound to be late and get caught up in the traffic.

His mother started to bemoan the fact that they had to spend a week in 'this Godforsaken awful place'. Grant was looking forward to being able to take Bruno for a walk; he liked his cousins' dog. His own home was strictly no pets, not even a fish.

Encounters

Emily and Grace walked down into the harbour hand in hand.

Emily loved the times when her daughter behaved like a nine-year-old rather than a nine-year-old going on fifteen who would be mortified to walk down their local high street holding hands with her mum.

Now that the sun was out from its hiding place behind the mist, the harbour was lit with the fresh morning light of a glorious May morning.

Fishing boats bobbed up and down on the water that was glistening in the sunshine; it promised to be a warm day.

The water looked really inviting, and Emily made a mental note to buy a local map that would identify some of the little coves that were more accessible to the holiday trade. Emily knew from her childhood that some of the coves could be quite dangerous.

She could remember going to somewhere called something or other steps or was it sands. They had set up their windbreaks and picnic rug and were all lying back and enjoying themselves when their mum had suddenly shot up and started to frantically gather all their stuff together, with the incoming tide only a couple of feet away and their exit route up the steps of the cliffs under water. From that day on, their dad had always double-checked the tide tables before they had ventured into any of the coves.

'Mummy, do you think they will be filming again this morning?'

'I am not sure, darling. We will have to wait and see when we get into the harbour.'

Emily remembered the guy that they had seen the night before, who had stopped them from going down into the harbour. She remembered that he had a nice smile and lovely eyes. Emily could feel herself blushing. She didn't even know the guy; he had looked the surfing type, or was that stereotyping? What did surfers look like? Normally they wore wetsuits. This guy had been dressed in scruffy jeans and a T-shirt; last year's tan was still visible. He had a stubble and sun-bleached blond hair, definitely not from a bottle.

Emily wasn't sure how much time actually was spent by the film crew in the harbour; she didn't suppose that they filmed much in the daytime, especially as it was the May half term. It would be busy, and they probably didn't need lots of visitors trying to observe what they were filming. She didn't anticipate that they could get much filming done with lots of visitors roaming around the place.

Reaching the harbour, they found the local store easily and purchased electric, milk, butter, and bread.

Leaving the store, they continued to walk down towards the harbour. Grace noticed that one shop sold knick-knacks for the beach.

Emily purchased a bucket, spade, and some flags for Grace and a kite for Max. She also bought both children a crabbing line; they loved crabbing when she could manage to get away for a few hours and take them to a local quay.

They continued down towards the harbour, and Emily pointed out that the building which was the tearoom fronted as a school in the *Doc Martin* series, and as they leant against the harbour wall, she pointed out that the house opposite was used for the surgery.

Grace had never seen the programme but was still excited at the prospect of being involved in an area that was famous and on TV, which would give her bragging rights in the playground.

Suddenly a voice behind them said, 'If you look at that little house going up the hill towards the surgery, that's the restaurant, or rather it's the garden we use for the restaurant.'

Emily turned round to the stranger.

'Oh, hi.' Emily could feel herself blushing as she realised that the man standing behind them was the guy who had stopped them the night before when they were walking down to the harbour—the guy she had just been daydreaming about. 'Thank you, we have only just arrived last night,' said Emily, slightly coyly.

'Yes, I remember you. Didn't you have a boy, your son, with you?'

Grace looked indignant. 'Max is lazy. He is still in bed, but Mummy and me have come to get some Cornish pasties for our breakfast.'

The man held out his hand.

'Simon, Simon Greene. I am one of the grips on the series. That means I do lots of organising of the running around, fetching and carrying, making sure everything is in the right place.'

Emily shook Simon's hand. 'Emily and Grace Vaughan.'

'Well, Emily and Grace, let me show you where the best pasties in Cornwall come from.'

Emily and Grace followed Simon down the hill.

Simon kept up a running commentary to Grace about all the shops, even pointing out the one owned by the wife of Lawrence Lhewellyn Bowan, who they watched from time to time on the Style channels. It felt comfortable walking alongside Simon, listening to his local knowledge.

When they reached the shop, Simon bid them farewell; he said he might see them around and left them to buy their breakfast.

'Mummy, he is a very nice man, isn't he, to show us where to go?'

Emily was just having a similar thought and agreed non-committally with her daughter's observations. Yes, a very nice man indeed, she thought, and a lovely smile and nice eyes. Emily felt light-headed; it was not something she had felt about a man for a long time.

Emily gave herself a metaphoric shake; she was not here for romance or even looking for it. She was here for quality time with her two children.

Emily bought them each a traditional Cornish pasty and a mix of different fruit-flavoured ones.

Walking back up the hill, Grace wondered where Simon was and again commented on what a nice man he was.

Emily daydreamed about what a lovely man he was; she remembered his smile from the previous night as well as his clear piercing blue eyes. He had made quite an impression on her, and by the sound of it, Grace was quite taken by him as well.

Emily hoped they might bump into him again. 'Maybe we could wander down to the pub tonight,' she thought.

Emily did not make a habit of chasing men; she had only had a handful of dates since her husband had left her, and they all pretty soon disappeared when they found out she had children. Not one had made an impact on her as Simon had. Simon knew already that she had the two children, but he had seemed to want to stay in conversation with them.

James

James had intended to get up early to be on the road as soon as possible, but he had worked late the previous night, having brought home a Chinese takeaway and the work he would normally do over the weekend. It had been nearly one o'clock this morning when he finally went to bed. It was now nine o'clock and traffic out of London was getting busy; he knew Tania would not be pleased. She had not been happy on the phone when he spoke to her before he left the office the night before; he had promised to come down early, and she was expecting him to find a solution to what she considered to be a problem.

James thought about his life. He had met Tania when she had moved up to London and moved in with her friend, who just happened to be the daughter of a work colleague. They had met one weekend when he had been invited round for a meal. Had it been love at first sight? Well, he had certainly fancied Tania like hell, and she had obviously fancied him. Tania had always had a good figure, even when pregnant; with her long legs, blonde hair, and large blue eyes, his mates thought him a lucky bugger. Two years later, she was pregnant with the first of the two boys. Once Adam had been born, Tania had refused to have any more children. She had said that it spoilt her figure, and she spent a month in, recovering from cosmetic surgery to get rid of the tummy and enhance her bust; both she decided were ruined with pregnancy.

James guessed Tania was what could be referred to as a trophy wife—very organised, well groomed, always in designer clothes, with matching or coordinating shoes and bags, normally Prada or Jimmy Choo. At parties, she was always the centre of attention, and it was the same if they went out or entertained at home. Little did people know to what cost.

Tania had insisted on a lavish five star wedding in a county house; she was spoilt, self-centred, and selfish and thought herself to be a WAG. He didn't know how her parents had paid for it; they gave Tania everything she demanded, unlike Emily who had a very low-key wedding the following year. James had his suspicions that the girls' parents had not been able to afford another lavish wedding. He had offered her father help towards paying for the wedding, but he was a proud man and would not accept help. He had paid for his own parents, his sister and brother, and their families to attend the wedding, plus his parents' outfits so that they did not feel like the poor relations. His cousin had referred to Tania as a cow, and Tania had overheard her saying that she was only marrying him for his money. Her parents had made his immediate family very welcome, and he knew his mum and dad had appreciated the Sunday dinner that his mother-in-law had cooked for them before they went home on the Sunday. Tania had been horrified when she had heard that her mother had done so; she was worried they might become friends!

Tania had refused to have anything to do with his family since; in fact, she rarely attended any family occasions on either sides of the family. At times, James was embarrassed by his wife's behaviour; she was very snobby, and the way she treated people whom she believed were beneath her was really dismissive. James's own parents were hard working, just like hers. His dad had been a manager for a local supermarket and his mother had worked in the local bakery. She still did a couple of mornings a week, and the boys loved the fact that Nana always had some forbidden cake in her kitchen, about which they never told their mother.

His sister now had three children and was unable to stay at home like Tania; she worked in the local pre-school ('not even a nursery' had been Tania's statement when he told her) to fit around her children's school term so that she was able to look after them. His brother-in-law's profession was that of a Plummer; he had his own business and worked hard to make a living. James knew that Tania looked down her nose at his family; she had really kicked up a fuss when he for once had put his foot down and insisted that his family and hers were to be invited to the boy's christening. All afternoon, she had ignored them and danced around their friends; the families had been placed at a table as far away from the house as possible. The caterers had been instructed to put round tables and pale blue tablecloths around the garden for guests to sit and eat at. Although James hated the way Tania treated his family, he also didn't like the way she had treated her mother and now her sister and father, but he knew that it was more than his life was worth to say anything. He had learnt early on in their relationship that he should keep his opinions to himself if he wanted his life to run smoothly. He would normally take the boys to see his own parents on weekends when Tania was at the spa or away with her girlfriends.

James often worried about his job due to the recent banking crisis. Tania loved to spend money; she would buy clothes and items for the house and engage interior designers to decorate the house. There was always something happening; she also spent thousands a year on spas, hair and entertaining. She insisted on having what she called the 'hired hands'; they spent more money than he cared to look at on entertaining and going out. Their food bills usually went through the roof. Tania bought mostly superior ready meals and had them delivered.

As he moved on to the M3, he knew that Tania was not going to be in the best of moods when he got there. Tania had never liked the rural town she had grown up in and hated returning there. She became uncomfortable and anxious when her life didn't run smoothly and to her exacting standards. She preferred to book into the hotel where they had gotten married than stay with her parents or sister. This always gave her an escape route and meant they only had to stay a short time.

James still could not understand Tania's behaviour when her mother had died; Tania had left everything to Emily. She had insisted they only turn up at the crematorium ten minutes before the service started; she had flounced inside and not acknowledged anyone apart from her sister and her father, to whom she said a curt hi. Straight after the service, they went back to her parents' house for the traditional tea and cake, and Tania had just spent about ten minutes in the house before she had insisted they leave. James had to drop her off at Bournemouth International Airport so that she could get a flight to Dublin and join her friends, who were there for a weekend to celebrate a birthday. James knew that Emily had been upset; he had overheard their brief exchange and that Emily had called her sister a selfish bitch. But Emily knew what her sister was like and never expected more from her. She had gratefully accepted the 500 pounds that James had slipped to her towards the funeral expenses. He guessed rightly that there would not be much spare cash in the bank to pay for things.

James was not sure that Tania could cope looking after her dad. He could remember his mum looking after his granddad and how difficult things had been. But from what Tania had said, having spoken to Emily, her father wasn't too bad. Maybe Tania was exaggerating the night before, when she rang him before he left the office. She certainly would not have the creature comforts she had at home; Emily didn't have a husband to provide for her.

Tania was not good at practical things; she was good at giving instructions to the people they employed. But helping an older person, well, James would reserve judgement and wait and see. He had already decided that if it looked like Mr P was being or going to be neglected, then it would be best to have him admitted into a rest home for a few days—anything to keep the peace. James liked his ordered life. Tania ran things very smoothly; the house was always spotless, clean, uncluttered, and chic as was Tania. The boys were always well behaved, and they could if they wanted take them anywhere. It had only occurred to him recently that they should start to come away on holidays with them, rather than make them stay at home with an au pair. When they were younger, they would be left with her parents also. Oh yes, they had always been useful for babysitting if it was school holidays and or if they interfered with Tania's plans, but Tania had always reasoned that they needed quality time together without having to amuse two boys, which could be stressful. James had promised them that he would take them skiing this winter; neither of the boys had been abroad with their parents, only going on school trips and a couple of times with school friends.

James knew Tania had felt blackmailed into looking after their father. But, secretly, he felt she also owed it to Emily. He had even offered to pay for a rest home when his father-in-law had first needed looking after, but Emily had been emphatic that she wanted to look after her dad herself and not leave him to strangers. James actually applauded her stance, though he would never voice his opinion out loud.

James guessed that one could call his wife cold. The children had mostly grown up with nannies and au pairs, then boarding school; there was not a lot he could do, with him working up to eighteen hours a day. In a fast-changing world of banking, you were expected to be seen putting in the hours. What with different time zones, sometimes when there was a crisis he slept for a couple of hours at his desk and never went home, so he was never really there to offer practical support and was just there to pay the bills. The children had grown up calling them Mummy and Daddy, but now even at ten and thirteen they still had to refer to them by the same. He knew the boys must be embarrassed in front of their friends, but Tania always had referred to her own parents as Mother and Father whereas Emily called them Mum and Dad as he did to his own parents. Tania thought 'Mummy and Daddy' sounded classy. Wasn't it what some of the nobility did?

As he moved on to the M27, his mobile rang; he glanced at it and saw Tania's mobile number and put it on to speaker.

'Hi, honey, how's it going?'

'It isn't.' Tania sounded like a petulant child, but James could handle her.

'Oh dear,' thought James with an inward groan, 'here goes.'

'I can't do this. He needs proper care, not Saint Emily.' Tania continued to fill James in on her version of events.

'Sweetheart, you should *not* be doing this,' soothed James. 'Can't we put him into a hospital or an old people's home?' James knew it was beyond his wife's capabilities to look after someone who needed personal care. His father-in-law would be much better cared for in a care/rest home for a week rather than by his elder daughter.

Tania continued to moan about Emily and how inconsiderate she was, and James listened, making soothing noises, for a further ten minutes until the boys interrupted her and wanted to talk to their father.

'Be there in about an hour, honey, and we will sort something out.'

An hour later, James turned into his sister-in-law's drive and was welcomed by his wife throwing herself into his arms.

'Darling, how are you?' James took her into his embrace as she burst into tears.

'It's sorted out. I have a taxi on its way. I have paid for a month in advance.'

'Woo, start again.' James continued to soothe her hair. He didn't understand what Tania was talking about.

'I have found my father a home where he should be! Oh, here's the taxi.'

James slightly bemused by the flood of events followed Tania back inside. 'Hi, Dad.' No response.

'You see, completely senile.'

Twenty minutes and a phone call later, they left Ringwood and headed for the hotel where they had got married, after James had promised Tania a massage and the boys a walk in the forest and a swim. They would stay there the night and go home the next morning; heaven knew what Emily would say when she found out.

James was slightly wary as Tania did not seem to know what the place was like or that she had not felt the need to go and take her father there herself, but this was Tania land. Tania did not confront anything that would make her look at her own emotions, except for the nice things in life.

Saturday

When Emily and Grace returned to the house, Max was up and had set the table for breakfast.

Emily thanked him; it was unusual for Max to do jobs around the house without being asked, and she was thankful that he had taken the initiative.

'Mum, I ended up washing the dishes before I set the table. They seemed greasy. Maybe we should wash them all when we wash up.' Max sounded really grown-up; Emily studied her twelve-year-old son. Emily was pleasantly surprised that her normally reluctant-to-do-'girl's work' son was able to identify that the dishes felt greasy. Nearly a year at secondary school had done wonders for Max's confidence and his common sense. The teachers were really pleased with his progress, and he was increasing his grades. Emily wondered if he would be an academic like her dad or sportier like his own father, although Emily remembered her son's reaction when he came home from a day out with his father. He had moaned because he had been taken to see Bournemouth play football at home. It had been raining and cold, and although Grace had seemed to enjoy it, Max had not found it enjoyable; maybe he was a 'Peters' at heart.

'It's not one of the best accommodations I know, but it's all I could afford.' Emily felt slightly bad that she had taken on face value the advertisement on the Internet and never questioned why it was so much cheaper than the others in the village; she had just presumed that it was not quite so close to the harbour and hence it did not create such a high rental. Neither of the children seemed unduly worried.

Max was more pragmatic. 'We won't be here much, will we? We are going exploring.'

Emily realised that she hadn't picked up the map that she had intended to buy.

'Right, breakfast, purchase a map, and then exploring.'

Both children grinned.

It only took an hour for them to eat, clear away their breakfast, and pack their bags with the new bits that Emily had purchased in the village along with their sun cream, sunglasses, towels, and hats. Whilst the children were doing this, Emily put together a quick picnic for them all to share later and took each of them a bottle of water out of the clean fridge.

Each of them had their own bag; this was something that Emily had always insisted on. From the time they could wear a backpack, when they went anywhere for the day, they all carried their fair share so that she wasn't left looking like a pack horse trailing behind. Some of her friends ended up with bags hanging off each arm, coats, or tops tied round their waists, and the ones that still had younger children in buggies always had an extraordinary number of things hanging from them, making it dangerous for them to lift the child out their buggies which always tipped up.

After a quick look round and opening all the little vents in the windows to enable the house to lose its musty smell, Emily carefully locked the door and wondered if it was really safe to leave the windows open. There were no window locks on the bigger windows, but she was sure that Mary was part of the neighbourhood watch and that there wasn't actually anything worth stealing inside the property and she certainly had nothing of value on her—just her handbag, camera, and mobile phone. Max had not been allowed to bring his or any of his other electric gadgets that he liked to play games on. Emily had wanted the children to spend quality time together and with her, without the constant beep of a Game Boy or a DS.

Suddenly remembering about her phone, she took it out of her bag, ready to turn it back on, then thought better of it and slipped it back again. 'Why spoil a good day?' She guessed (correctly but was yet to find this out) that by now her sister would have left a message, having a good moan if not about their dad then definitely about the dog.

Emily and the children set off down the road towards the harbour. 'Look, Mum,' said Grace, 'there's Gwen.' Grace started to wave at the older lady, who in turn waved back.

'Hello, folks,' said Gwen as she spotted them all coming towards her. 'Off out, are we? How have you settled in?'

'I had to wash up all the pots, cups, and cutlery before we had breakfast.' This was an indignant outburst from Max before Emily could say anything to stop him. Gwen looked slightly embarrassed, but Emily noticed that her own cottage didn't look dissimilar to the one they were renting. Gwen raised an eyebrow at Emily.

'Well, it's not quite like we anticipated, as it was shown on the Internet,' Emily found herself saying. 'The house does seem to need a bit more of a clean.'

Gwen started to fidget. 'I am so sorry, but with my mum being in the home and the distance to Truro, I really was going to give it a good going-over. But I haven't had the time. I will ask George to come and mow the lawns.'

Emily smiled. She liked Gwen and didn't want any ill feelings between them; she could empathise with her situation. 'That would be lovely. We would like to have a BBQ one evening, and you are most welcome to join us.'

Gwen looked really pleased. 'That will be lovely. Haven't been to a BBQ for ages.'

Emily and the children said their goodbyes and walked on down towards the harbour, Emily thinking that she would also ask Mary to come to this BBQ that she had just decided to give! Both the children chatted as they decided on what they would like to eat at the BBQ. Emily did quite a lot of BBQs in the summer at home, and they always tried to have alternatives for sausages and burgers, or if they did have sausage and burgers, these were sourced at the local farm shop or Emily made the burgers herself. Emily enjoyed entertaining both in summer and winter and her cakes were always in demand at school, whether for the staffroom or the cake stall.

As they walked down the hill, Emily remembered the map that she wanted to buy; halfway down, Grace started to point out with an authoritative voice, showing her knowledge of the various buildings that Simon had shown her earlier. It was nice for Grace to find she was able to tell her brother something that he didn't already know. As they reached the building that doubled as the school house, Emily noticed that there was a shop attached to it, which looked as though it might sell the sort of map she was looking for. Emily found an old 'sea dog' behind the counter; she explained what she was looking for whilst the children wandered around, looking wide-eyed at the array of interesting items he had on offer. There were all kinds of items associated with the sea from wooden ships and sea gulls to toffee and biscuits with Port Isaac written on the lids. Paying for her map which included head land walks, Emily called the children to her.

Once in the harbour, the children were delighted to find that the tide was out, and they wanted to go exploring in the pools left by the outgoing tide. Emily set down their stuff near some rocks so that she had somewhere to sit. Leaning back with her face turned to the sun, she thought how relaxing it was not to have to worry about time and to just enjoy the moment. Emily glanced up to check if the children were OK. Both were engrossed in looking in rock pools, placing items in the bucket that she had brought for Grace earlier. Max was instructing Grace on each item that they found. Looking up, he noticed Emily looking at them; both children came running over. 'Look, Mum,' exclaimed an excited Grace, 'look, we have caught a prawn.'

'I keep telling her it's a shrimp,' said Max. 'Can we go up to the shop and get a net if I look out to Grace?'

Emily considered his request; there were hardly any cars up and down the narrow street to the harbour, and apart from when they rounded the corner, she would be able to see them all the way. At nearly twelve, Max was a sensible lad and was used to walking to school on his own since he had started secondary school in September.

'OK. But please keep an eye on your sister.' She turned to Grace. 'Listen to what Max says.'

Both the children picked up their wallets from their bags and headed off in the direction of the shop. Emily sat back once more to enjoy the surroundings, looking up at the small village that sat above the harbour and the grassy slope of the cliff that ran up the other side. She could see the children peering over the wall, waving at her. This was another world, much slower and more relaxed than the town where they lived, and although they only lived a short drive from the sea or the New Forest, it always seemed so busy. Take the market day in the town where her aunt lived; there was always the pushing and shoving of people, dogs and buggies, and Emily avoided it as much as she could. She loved Lymington with its quaint harbour and the cobbled quay, and the children loved to go crabbing there but never on a Saturday; it was just so busy. Emily loved to go and see her aunt (her mum's sister); recently she had not been able to go much because of her dad. She tried to go one weekday each holiday when her dad was in the day centre. She loved to start at the top of the town and wander right down the high street to the quay and back up the other side. It was lovely. There were a lot of independent shops and coffee shops; she and her aunt always avoided larger chain store coffee shops and used one of the many small independent ones. The children loved to catch the ferry to the Isle of Wight and roam around Yarmouth. Last time they had caught the open top bus to Alum bay and gone to look at the different coloured sands, but even that had changed from her childhood memories. Emily remembered just going down on a chair lift to the beach and collecting coloured sands and filling a glass shape with it. Now it was a theme park. At least here in Port Isaac, it was the same as she remembered it to have been.

Emily decided that when the children returned she would take herself into the cafe behind her; if she sat in the corner, she would be able to see the children from there and keep an eye on them.

The children returned each with a net. Max made sure that Grace returned her wallet back into her bag properly before he allowed her to go back to the rock pool. Emily sat watching him, smiling to herself, pleased that her son was so gentle and kind to his sister; they did actually get on really well, but Emily knew that there would soon be a time when Max would start to consider his sister a pest. Three years' difference wasn't that great when you were only ten or eleven, but wait till he was thirteen or fourteen.

Emily explained to the children where she was going and where she was going to sit. Moving across to the cafe, she was annoyed to see a man sitting at the table with his back to her. She felt cheated; it was her table, the one she had chosen to sit at. She could see the waitress approach the man with a tray; as the man looked up, she saw that it was Simon. Emily entered the cafe, trying not to look at Simon. She didn't want him to think he was being stalked; their paths did seem to be crossing today. She took a seat a couple of tables away, where she could still see the children. The waitress approached her.

'Hi, what can I get you?' she asked, holding her pen poised above her little pad.

'Can I have a latte please?' Emily replied, looking up and smiling at the young girl.

'Hello, we meet again.' Simon had looked up when she had ordered and recognised her as she sat there. 'Would you like to join me?'

Emily smiled. Simon thought to himself, 'She has such an illuminated face when she smiles. She has a warm smile that reaches her eyes.'

'Yes, please, I had chosen that table from the beach so that I could watch the children. It will give me a much better view.' Emily realised this sounded rude and quickly added, hoping he wouldn't realise it was an afterthought, 'It will be nice to have someone to talk to whilst I sit here.'

The waitress came and placed the latte in front of Emily and left the little docket on the table. Simon quickly picked it up and said, 'Add it to my bill.'

'No, it's OK. I will pay for mine. I can't expect you to pay.' Emily was slightly embarrassed.

'No worries. The company has an account. I am sure one extra latte won't get noticed.' Simon smiled at her.

Emily settled back with her latte and turned her head so that she could see the children. There were a few minutes of awkward silence before Simon started the conversation.

'So how old are they?' Simon inclined his head towards Max and Grace.

'Max is nearly twelve and Grace is nine years old, going on nineteen.' Emily gave a little laugh.

'Oh, tell me about it.' Emily felt her stomach turn over. He was married with children! 'My sister is always telling me that my nieces are teenagers in waiting, and they are only three and five years old.'

Emily felt relief and then wondered to herself, 'What is the matter with me? I have only spoken to him three times and here I am getting upset because he might be married.'

'So no children yourself then?' she heard herself saying.

'No, no children or significant other,' Simon replied, his eyes twinkling in the midday sunshine. 'What about your significant other? There must be one somewhere, the children's father?'

Emily found herself explaining about her marriage, divorce, and her father all in one sentence. She did not say anything about Tania, feeling that to do so would make her sound bitchy.

Simon listened, and Emily found herself relaxing as her whole life story seemed to pour out of her. Simon was a good listener and made eye contact when necessary so that Emily didn't feel self-conscious about her life history.

Emily was brought out of her memories by the sound of children running across the harbour, calling her. 'Mum, we are hungry,' cried Grace. 'Can we have lunch, please?'

Emily started to gather up her bag and sunglasses. She turned and smiled at Simon. 'Thanks for the coffee and listening. I hope I didn't bore you.'

'The pleasure was all mine. Maybe I will see you in the pub later. It's where everyone congregates in the evening.' Simon's eyes met hers, and for a moment, Emily experienced a fusion of something. Could it be excitement?

Emily shepherded her children out of the restaurant, asking them to go and collect all their belongings. Looking at her watch, she realised it was only half past eleven; it was a bit early for lunch as later they would be wanting snacks and then not eat their tea that night. Emily looked at the signposts that were at the corner.

'Come on, let's walk up here. We will go past the surgery for the programme and then we can walk up the hill and have our picnic looking out across the harbour.'

The children started up the hilly path in front of Emily. When they reached the house used in the programme, there was a clear notice saying that it was only a front and that a family actually lived in the house. Emily moved the children past it, explaining to them what the notice actually meant.

Emily and the children made it to the top of the hill and set up their picnic, looking out to sea. Max asked what the bay below them was. Emily dug out her new map. 'Port Gaverne.' Both children crowded round the map. 'It says here that at low tide it's one of the safest places for children to play in North Cornwall.'

'Can we go down please?' Both children looked at her appealingly.

Four hours later after the tide had started to come in, Emily and the children returned to the harbour, debating what to have for tea. Max wanted fish and chips and Grace and Emily were suggesting salad, when once again a voice behind them offered advice.

'If you want fish and chips, you need to go to Padstow.' Emily recognised Simon's voice instantly.

Emily turned round, smiling. 'Do you always pop up behind people or were you lying in wait?'

Simon looked slightly apologetic. 'Sorry, didn't mean to butt in, but truly if you want great fish and chips you will need to go to Padstow.'

Both children looked up at Emily expectantly. 'Not tonight. I was looking earlier at the map and thought we could hire bikes either tomorrow or Monday and ride along the Camel trail that ends or starts at Padstow, so we can get them then.'

Simon turned back to Emily. 'Now you have a problem, don't you?' Emily raised her eyebrows in question. 'What are you going to do for tea now?'

'Yuk, it's got to be salad.' There was a groan from Max.

'I would like it if you would all join me for supper in the pub,' Simon asked.

Emily was slightly confused. Had she heard right? Had Simon just suggested taking them all for supper? She was surprised, as she was more used to men running a mile when she mentioned children, and here was someone she had only met by accident a couple of times offering them all supper.

'Mum.' Emily felt a tug on her trouser leg. Grace was looking up at the wonder on her face. 'Mum, Simon says he wants us to go to supper with him. Can we?'

Emily pulled herself together. 'Er, um, you don't want us to stop your fun. Surely you have other things to do.'

Simon smiled, 'Meet you at seven thirty.' He raised his hand in salute and walked off up the hill the same way from where Emily had just come, not giving Emily any time to argue.

'Cor, Mum, I think you have pulled,' laughed Max.

'Max! Where on earth did you hear things like that?' Emily was slightly shocked to hear her young son suggest such a thing. Inwardly, Emily wondered if her son's observations were true. Had she indeed pulled as he so delicately put it?

Emily and the children had a lovely evening in the pub; after eating a really nice supper, with the children having sausages and mash again, the talk was relaxed. The children were able to go outside and watch the boats now that the tide was in. Simon explained that he was working in the area for the second series of the programme and that he had rented a house nearby with three other crew members. He told Emily about the different places they could visit; Emily found she had to remind him that they were only there until the following Friday morning and how she had to get home because of her sister who was looking after their father. Emily felt a twinge of guilt; her mobile was still in her bag, and she hadn't turned it on all day. Pushing the thought to the back of her mind, she promised to turn it on the following morning. The children started to squabble, then Grace started to show signs of becoming tired. Emily thanked Simon for a very nice evening and meal and prompted the children to say thank you. Emily declined Simon's offer to walk them up the hill and said good night.

The Aftermath

The following morning James crept out of bed at seven thirty; quietly picking up his own stuff, he went to the boys' room along the hotel corridor. He let himself in and used their shower before waking them up to go for breakfast. James decided over breakfast that he would take the boys for a swim and then see if Tania was awake. At ten o'clock, Tania was still sound asleep. James got the boys to gather their bits together, and after leaving a note on the pillow, telling Tania the bill was paid, he and the boys headed back to London.

Tania woke around ten thirty. She had slept well; the bed was comfortable and the room dark. She vaguely wondered where James and the boys were, but headed for the bathroom for a long soak in the bath with the quality bath cosmetics that are always complimentary in hotels.

She wrapped herself in a luxurious white towel, and then as she was drawing back the curtains, she saw the note on the pillow. Her first thoughts after reading the note were 'good peace and quiet'. She rang room service and ordered Danish pastries and coffee with fresh orange juice. Next, she rang the spa and booked a neck and shoulder massage; she knew the long journey back would give her tension.

An hour and a half later, Tania called the concierge and asked for her suitcase to be taken to her car. As soon as Tania hit the A35 towards the motorway, she started to relax; she was going home. She was leaving behind what she always thought of as the outback and heading back to all her mod cons and domestic help, with beauty and shopping on tap as well as decent restaurants and coffee shops—not that the hotel restaurant last night had not been excellent; it was one of the many reasons she always insisted on staying there.

The Nursing Home

Mrs Dorothy Grey, Dotty to her friends, had owned Sunshine Rest Home near Bournemouth for twenty-five years and she thought she had probably seen and heard most things, but this morning having returned from a day off, she was listening to the sister in charge telling her all about a new resident. There was also a message from a Marie, a home carer, enquiring about Mr Peters. It seemed that his daughter had sent him in a taxi with hardly any clothes or medication the day before, paying in advance for a month's stay.

The sister was explaining the situation and Dotty could tell she was pretty mad. 'Sorry, but she sounded like a real hard cow. Her sister who is the main carer has gone on holiday and left her in charge, and Miss La De Da couldn't cope.' The sister sniffed. 'I think you should contact Social Services. They need to know what is going on.'

Dotty smiled calmly. 'I know, dear, it sounds so distressing, but let me speak to the home carer and see what she has to say. His bill is paid, so at the moment he has not been completely abandoned.'

Normally Sundays were quiet. Some residents went out with their relatives. That day the other residents were being taken after lunch to Compton Acres, a local garden attraction, and would have afternoon tea there; it also meant a bit of a treat for the staff who accompanied them. The rest home calculated the cost into the fee charged for the resident, so the staff got it free. 'Not many perks in this kind of job,' thought Dotty. Dotty was pleased she had employed an entertainment organiser as it seemed to benefit the residents and they had lots of new and stimulating things to do. Although some of the staff seemed to think that some relatives did not come as often, they knew they were not missed so much. Mrs Grant had been overheard to tell her son and his children to 'bugger off' the other day when they were going on a mystery cream tea tour.

Dotty looked at the number in front of her and dialled. Twenty minutes later, Dotty was explaining to the sister how Mr Peters had ended up in Sunshine Rest Home.

'Told you she was a harsh cow.' The sister was adamant she would not give Tania any slack.

'Well.' Dotty smiled again; she also didn't like the sound of Tania, and having spoken at length to Marie, she was surprised at how 'chalk and cheese', as Marie had put it, the two sisters sounded. 'The home carer is going to bring some more clothes and essentials, plus his tablets and care plan.'

Even Marie had been amazed that Mr P (as she referred to him) had not come with his tablets; she said, 'Good job nothing was life-threatening.' She had told Dotty that she did not want to ring Emily as she deserved her break, and as Tania had actually paid for the rest home, she felt that it might be best to wait till Emily came home before breaking the news unless 'the cow has told her'.

Dotty sat with a cup of coffee in her office and wondered how one daughter could be so caring whilst the other was obviously cold. She had agreed with Marie that it was best for all to allow Emily to have a break with her two children, and they could sort out what was going to happen when she returned. It sounded to Dotty that Emily was the kind of woman who would insist that her dad went back home, but maybe Dotty could explain to her about respite care.

Sunday

Sunday morning arrived bright and clear. Emily stretched and wondered what time it was. Looking at the little travel clock she had brought with her, she could see that it was only six thirty but she was wide awake. Throwing back the bed covers, she stretched and jumped out of bed. Normally on a Sunday morning, her dad would wake her around six o'clock, when she would pop on the TV and then lie back in bed and try to sleep until the local church bells would wake her up at about quarter to eight. She decided to go downstairs and make herself a cup of coffee. Emily padded down the stairs and filled the kettle; whilst she waited for it to boil she walked into the small lounge. Looking around, she realised it was as dreary as the rest of the cottage. The night before, she had cleaned the bathroom before both children took a shower and then again afterwards before she had sunk into a long and leisurely bath. It was not something that she had time to do at home; she was always aware that she could be needed to attend to her dad. 'Shame,' she had thought the night before, 'I should have brought some candles with me.' But she had enjoyed the luxury of a glass of wine and a bar of chocolate and had a good read.

Emily threw open the windows and decided that she would do a little cleaning. Taking her coffee with her, she gathered up the cleaning products and a bowl of soapy water; she started to dust the lounge, using a wet cloth. Emily worked methodically for an hour. Straightening up, she looked around, pleased with the result, and then in a fit of energy she decided to strip the loose covers off the small sofa, armchair, and the cushions, justifying this activity in her head, 'Well, you don't know who or what have been on them.' She walked through to the kitchen and deposited them into the washing machine as she heard movements upstairs. Emily knew that her cleaning bordered on OCD behaviour, but ever since Max had contacted gastroenteritis when he was three months old she had been fanatical about keeping the house clean; what with the dog and now her dad living with them, it was important that her house was spotlessly clean. Anyway, she felt sorry for Gwen, who was obviously struggling to stay afloat, and as the children were still asleep, she had nothing else to do. She didn't want to sit in the chairs to read her book with them looking like they did.

Emily started to lay the table for breakfast, thinking as she put out the plates and bowls that she would tackle the windows and net curtains later. She did feel sorry for Gwen; she was not that young, and she had to dash about, trying to look out for her mother and keep two houses going. Making the long round trip to Truro on a regular basis must be very tiring and perhaps didn't give her much time for maintenance on either property.

The children arrived bleary-eyed due to sleep, both still in their pj's just like any other Sunday morning. Max wanted to turn on the TV, but Emily reminded him they were on holiday and needed to sit down and work out where they wanted to go that day.

Grace said she liked the idea of hiring bikes and going to Padstow. Emily reached for the map so that they could all see what the alternatives were. Max pointed out the Camel trail with his finger. 'Look, it starts here at Bodmin and finishes up in Padstow. Cor, it looks a long way.'

Emily explained that they would only be able to start at Padstow or Wadebridge as they would need to hire bicycles for each of them. They again consulted the map and the surrounding advertisements. Emily saw that they could rent bikes at either end and also leave them safely locked up whilst they looked round in either of the towns.

Grace looked concerned, 'But we have to start in Wadebridge or we won't get our fish and chips. You promised, Mum.'

Emily wasn't about to break her promise and confirmed their plans, looking at the map and wondering if both children and herself would be able to complete the whole thing. The map said it was eighteen miles from Bodmin to Padstow, but they would be starting in Wadebridge and they would also have to do the return journey. The suggested time was nearly three hours each way!

Emily suggested that they all went upstairs, had a wash, and got ready and then she would ring and reserve bikes for them all. As the children scampered upstairs, there was a knock at the door. Emily opened it, expecting either Gwen or Mary to be on the step and was surprised to see Simon.

'Hi, I thought you might like a guide for your trip to Padstow. You did say you intended to go for a bike ride along the Camel trail, didn't you?'

Emily, slightly surprised at the fact that he was standing on her doorstep and even more surprised that he was offering to spend a day with them, looked bemused; she was also conscious of the fact that she was only dressed in a tracksuit bottom and old T-shirt and had not bothered to brush her hair when she had got up. That coupled with the last couple of hours of cleaning meant she looked a mess.

Simon's smile slipped slightly. 'Er, maybe you want to spend the time with the children and not have a stranger in tow.'

Emily quickly gathered her thoughts. 'Sorry, you took me by surprise. Please come in.' She stood back to allow him to pass. 'We are just getting ready, and yes, we would love company. I wasn't being rude, just didn't expect you. Go through to the kitchen whilst I change and hurry the children along. Make yourself a coffee.'

Emily bounced up the stairs as Simon made his way into the kitchen. Neither child seemed bothered when Emily explained that Simon would be coming with them, and Max proclaimed it to be 'cool'.

Emily took ten minutes to freshen up and change; she wished she had more time to take a shower, but considering they would be riding bikes all day, she tied her hair up in a ponytail and decided that she would have a nice long bath again later. Maybe in Padstow or Wadebridge she would find some scented candles and nice bath foam.

Once she was ready, she ran down the stairs and noticed that Simon had washed up their breakfast things for her. When she thanked him, he reassured her that it was no bother as he had been waiting. Emily quickly emptied the covers from inside the washing machine, explaining about the certain lack of cleanliness in the house, before heading into the garden to use the line. By nine thirty, they were all ready to pile into the large van that Simon had borrowed. In the back were four bikes.

'I hope they are the right size for you both.' Simon looked at Grace and Max. 'I borrowed them from a friend and promised we would take good care of them. Their children are the same age and about the same size as you both.'

Both children and Emily thanked him for his thoughtfulness. Emily explained that she had intended to hire their bikes, but Simon pointed out that it was very expensive.

Simon drove carefully towards Wadebridge, having suggested that it was better to start there. Emily and the children agreed that they had also decided to go that way. Emily mused that they were both of a similar frame of mind and had similar ideas and thoughts.

Once they had parked the van, Emily insisted on purchasing the parking ticket. Then they moved off, after Simon had adjusted the seat slightly for Grace.

They rode along the old railway line at a steady pace. Max had set his watch to see how long it would take. The path was fairly flat, but they needed to watch out for potholes; it was still relatively early for walkers and families, but there were quite a few other bike riders out. Every twenty minutes, they stopped to have a drink and to catch their breaths and admire the view. Simon was quite knowledgeable about the wild life and was able to show the children the different birds and name them for them, something that Emily would have struggled to do. He also spent time helping both children get the best possible pictures with their cameras. She had used a bit of her dad's pension to buy them one each for their birthdays. Her mum had always bought useful but also interesting presents, and she had promised her that she would continue to do the same all the time her dad was still here so that the children's life was kept as near to normal as possible.

It took them nearly three hours to ride into Padstow, and by this time they were passing lots of cyclists and walkers coming in from the opposite direction; all of them were feeling hungry and looking forward to their fish and chips. Simon led the way to the large warehouse, where for a small charge they were able to leave their bikes in safety.

Simon showed them the way to the front of the dock area, where the row of shops faced across the estuary towards Rock. Emily could hear him explaining to the children that Rick Stein, the television chef, owned some restaurants in the town and that his fish and chips were brilliant. He had obviously had some before. Emily insisted that she bought their lunch as Simon had supplied the bikes. All four of them took their bags of fish and chips and sat with their feet dangling over the side of the harbour wall munching away. Herring gulls were flying around, squawking, wanting their share. Grace dropped a chip and a flock descended on them, making a commotion whilst the children laughed; neither was scared. They had seen seagulls before, maybe not so big, but still they were used to them at home.

Once they had eaten and placed the wrappings in the bin, they decided to go and look around the harbour. It was busy; an ice cream van stood at one end with a queue. Emily suggested they could have one on the way back. People were milling around, looking in shop windows; the pace was slow, but the children and Emily were interested in all the coming and going as they slowly made their way round the harbour wall.

Emily was beginning to remember coming here as a child; she could remember going up the hill on the other side of the harbour, just like lots of people seemed to be doing that day. They had walked up past the monument at the top and followed the path down to a long sandy beach. She seemed to remember that when the tide went out it never seemed to be that deep, but maybe that was just her memory playing tricks on her. What she could remember well was watching the wind surfers and power boats going up and down the inlet.

Max and Grace watched boats coming in and out of the harbour; this was a small fishing community and boats were coming back with their catch. It was Simon who noticed a sign for 'Black Tor Ferry' connecting Padstow to Rock on the other side and suggested that they take a trip across as the beach was sandy. Both children once again looked at Emily expectantly; she realised that as she had not hired the bikes she could afford a small ferry trip and still come out not having spent what she had budgeted for that day. They became excited at the prospect of a trip across the water and joined the short queue waiting for the next ferry.

The ferry was busy, and they had to crowd up against each other to make room for everyone to sit down. Emily was quite aware of Simon sitting pressed up beside her; their thighs were pressed close together and he had his arm draped across her back so he could slightly turn and see where they were heading. Every so often, his fingers trailed across her shoulder. She found that she was quite enjoying this physical contact with a man; it had been a long while, and this all felt so comfortable.

When they climbed off the boat at Rock, the children straight away headed for a piece of sand and started to dig with their hands. Two minutes later, they were joined by a dog, a brown Labrador, but it suddenly reminded Emily of Bruno and that her mobile phone was still turned off in her bag; she delved inside and pulled it out. Turning it on, she found herself apologising to Simon, who reassured her by bringing out his own from his jeans pocket and telling her that he never turned it off. Then he suggested that they should swap numbers.

As the phone came to life, it started to bleep. Emily had sixteen missed calls and three texts; quickly panicking and reading the log, she noted they were all either from her sister's mobile or from her own house phone, one from Wendy, and her voicemail. Breathing deeply to calm her nerves, she dialled her voicemail number. 'You have three new messages. Message one: "Emily, Emily where the hell are you, I can't cope." Message left at . . .' It had been left at three o'clock the day before. What had Tania done? What had her dad done? Was he ill? Emily listened to the other two messages from Tania; it was obvious that she could not cope with their father and was at her wit's end, and she had only been there for less than twenty-four hours when she made the first call. The other two suggested that if Emily did not return her calls Tania would be looking at putting their father into a home. Wendy's call was much more enlightening and in some respects more reassuring; she explained what had happened earlier in the day and that Tania had told her to leave the house. She had also been told that her sister had moved their father into a rest home; she went on to explain that Marie was sorting everything out at their end and not to worry. She had left her love before ringing off, telling her Bruno was now on holiday with them.

Emily felt tears welling up in her eyes. Why could she not even have a week's break? Why was her sister such a spoiled brat? There had never been much closeness between them while growing up as Tania was always the needy one and Emily much more self-sufficient. Emily apologised once more to Simon and briefly outlined the situation, explaining she needed to ring her sister. He suggested that he would go and look for a drink for them all whilst she made contact.

Emily dialled Tania's mobile, realising she had not looked at her texts but guessed they would be similar to the voice message. Tania answered almost straight away, '*Where* the bloody hell have you been? I have left you loads of messages. I couldn't cope, and he wet himself twice and then turned on the empty kettle. He's a danger to himself and to everyone else.' Tania took a breath. 'I don't know how you have put up with it so long. Well, you won't any longer.' Emily felt the hairs on her neck stand on end and then felt some form of relief when Tania continued, 'He is now in a rest home in Bournemouth, and we will pay for him to stay there. No one can be expected to look after a senile old man.'

'Tania, you have done what?' Emily found herself exploding, and both children and Simon who had just returned with two cokes and two coffees looked at her. 'You have put our father in a home!' Emily could feel the tears coursing down her cheeks; both children came and stood beside her as she knelt on the beach.

'You heard me. He is in a rest home near Bournemouth called "Sunshine". It was the only one with an immediate place.'

'Heavens above, Tania, did you not stop to wonder why it might have a place? Did you go there and see what it was like? Was Dad happy when you left him?' Emily bombarded her sister with questions.

'Er . . . I don't know. I never actually took him there.' Quick to defend herself, Tania added, 'James would not be happy if he had wet in our new car.'

'Tania, let me get this straight. You have put Dad into a rest home in Bournemouth that you know nothing about and you didn't even take him. How did he get there?'

'I didn't let him walk, if that's what you think. I put him in a taxi.' Tania started to sound defensive.

'Where are you now?' Emily wanted to strangle her sister among other things, but most of all she was worried about her father; he would be confused and frightened and God only knows how the people at the home were treating him. 'Do you have a phone number for this home?'

'I am at my local spa. I just had to come straight here. I have had a long drive home this morning, so no, I don't have the phone number on me.' Emily found herself looking at her phone screen and pressing the disconnect button. This was not the first time she had been angry with her sister, but this was the first time she could remember herself being so angry that she felt she actually hated her sister. She sat staring at it for a while.

'Emily, Emily,' she heard Simon's concerned voice through the fog that had seemed to have entered her head. 'I have got the gist. Your sister has put your father into a home which she hasn't seen, but why?'

Emily sent the children off to see if they could find some shells whilst she quickly explained to Simon what had happened and how worried she was about the situation. Simon withdrew his own phone from his pocket and started to tap on the screen. 'Here we are. There is a Sunshine Rest Home near Bournemouth listed here.' He handed the screen to Emily; he had a Blackberry which he had used to bring up the Internet and search for the rest home. It did look and sound friendly and had a good report from the local authority. The residents in the pictures looked happy. Emily typed the phone number into her phone and waited for the ringing tone before handing back Simon his phone with a watery smile.

A pleasant voice answered at the end of the line, and Emily explained who she was and asked how her father was. The woman explained that she would call the owner to speak to Emily. Ten minutes later, Emily came off the phone looking brighter and less worried. Both children still looked concerned. 'Well, he has settled in well. The reason they had a room was that another resident had gone into hospital and they had been asked to re-let his room. Although they had a waiting list, Tania had insisted that she needed somewhere right away and they had been concerned for Dad's safety. She had in fact been so concerned she had wanted the manager to ring Social Services.' Emily explained, 'The supervisor had wanted the manager to contact Social Services, but as the room was paid for at the moment, there was no need and they had spoken to Marie.' Now that Emily had explained the situation and made an appointment to go in as soon as they were back in the Bournemouth area on the following Friday, the owner, a Mrs Grey 'but call me Dotty', had assured Emily she would sort things out until then. Her father was eating, and the nurse had taken him for a walk round the garden, where he had pointed out the various plants to her. Also, he was going on a trip that afternoon. Emily had asked Dotty to be sure to include him in any trips as he would miss the care centre and the children and that she would sort out payment for extras when she got back.

Emily was much more relieved now and quietly drank her coffee, leaning against Simon; she had not realised he was sitting beside her and had put his arm around her shoulders. Emily felt she needed to explain to Simon what her sister was really like and the history between them both. Simon was very empathic; he hated women like Tania and would normally spot them a mile off, although . . . that story could keep for another day.

'You know, if that was my brother or sister doing that to my mum and dad, I don't think I would be able to keep my hands off them,' Simon said, offering his own support. 'Come on, let's join those kids and bury them in the sand.' Simon brought Emily back to reality; yes, she would continue to enjoy her holiday, and she would not let her sister spoil it any more. Simon seemed generally angry on her behalf. Dotty had said she could ring any time and that she would bring him home on Friday.

The rest of the afternoon passed pleasantly; they took the return boat to Padstow at four o'clock and then walked back and collected the bikes. By the time, they pulled up outside the cottage it was nearly eight thirty and both children were exhausted. Emily and the children thanked Simon for a lovely day; she thought about inviting him in, but she ached because of riding the bike and was looking forward to a long hot bath; she had found the candles and bath foam when they were in Padstow and there was some wine left in the fridge.

Simon's Story

As Simon drove home that night, he pondered over the situation he was beginning to find himself in. Simon Andrew Greene was twenty-seven years old; he knew he was probably younger than Emily and of course she had kids, both lovely polite kids. But the big plus was, that after the affair he had, had last year Emily wasn't married. Maybe, he thought, he should have opened up and told Emily about 'her' when he had the opportunity as they had sat on the beach, but then it would have given her the wrong impression and then they would never get to know each other. Emily had relaxed once she had come off the phone to the rest home. She had been reassured and had quietly drunk her coffee, leaning against Simon. He didn't know if she had realised as he had sat beside her and put his arm around her shoulders, but she had not objected. Emily had explained to Simon what her sister was really like and the history between them both. Simon was very empathic; he hated women like Tania and would normally spot them a mile off, although he had lowered his guard last year with unwanted consequences.

Simon lived what his grandmother had called a 'charmed life'; he was the youngest of three children. Both his parents were professionals, and while growing up, all three children had been indulged, some would say spoilt, although from what Emily had said he had had a much more grounded childhood than her nephews did. He did reflect that most of what he and his brother, Matt, and sister, Pam, had was probably through guilt on their parents' behalf to make up for the long hours they both worked. As a child, the children spent most holidays in Cornwall, staying with their grandparents who lived just outside of Tintagel, whilst their parents stayed in Brighton and continued to work. Both his parents where surgeons; his mother was an ear, nose, and throat surgeon and his father was a neurologist.

Every summer, they took three weeks off work and took their three children away for quality time as a family and to probably give the grandparents a break. The only help that his mother did have at home and still had was a cleaner; she did all the cooking, washing, and childcare in term time herself whilst his father took care of the garden. He always said it relaxed him after working all week.

As they had gotten older, their parents still liked them all to go on big family holidays together, but now they had bought a villa in the South of France and the family went there from Easter to the end of October. Having retired, his parents loved to spend the summer there but always spent Christmas in England. His father said Christmas was not meant to be warm! Simon was intending to spend the last week of August over there this year. He would drive down so he could take all his water sports gear and enjoy the sunshine.

He had never heard his parents complain that he had wasted his education—a 2:1 from Plymouth University in marine biology, but after four years at uni and after all the years spent at school and college, he had decided he needed time out to recharge his batteries and take stock of his life; that had been three years ago.

He had come back to North Cornwall, which he had loved as a child. Both his grandparents were now gone; they had left all three grandchildren a nest egg. One night in the pub, he had been talking to some guys about surfing and the local area; they had needed his local knowledge and liked him, so there and then he had been offered him the job, and he was happy with the life he led. Did he want to complicate it with a new relationship?

His job role as a key grip meant that he was in charge of all the people who moved anything. He was the boss of all the individuals who moved scenery and cameras and set up and took down the scaffolding on which the lights, microphones, etc. were hung. The job had its perks too; it had led to him meeting plenty of pretty girls, and then last year he had met Mariana.

Simon arrived home; he looked out of his windscreen. He was surprised that he was home; he couldn't remember the journey from Emily's cottage and sat for a few minutes in the van. He would return the bikes tomorrow morning; now he wanted to hear Emily's voice again, have a hot shower, a drink, and fall into bed. Once inside, Simon took himself straight off to his bathroom and jumped in the shower; he was a fit and active guy, but riding bikes that day he realised he had used muscles he hadn't used for ages. Once showered with a drink in his hand, he made the call to Emily. They talked about the day; she thanked him for taking them and told him how much all three of them had enjoyed themselves. He was worried about her and asked her if she was OK. She told him that she had spoken to the 'home' again and her dad was settled and had enjoyed his afternoon out; she certainly seemed happier with the situation but was still furious with her spoilt sister. They arranged to spend the day together on Tuesday and said goodbye.

Simon decided to go straight to bed; he didn't fancy sitting around that night with the other guys who shared the house. But once he turned out the light, he was unable to settle down to sleep. He had awoken memories that he would rather leave in the past.

Wow, what a monumental cock-up his relationship with Mariana had been; she was older than him. At thirty-nine, she was a bored housewife, living in a sleepy Cornish village when she was used to the cosmopolitan lifestyle of Italy, her home country. She and her husband had recently moved to Cornwall after ten years in Italy. She had a successful husband, and with her two children away at school Monday to Friday, she had nothing to do. He had been approached by her one day when he had gone over to see his grandmother in Tintagel. He had stopped off at a pub on his way home for a drink and some supper. He had been flattered that this sophisticated woman wanted to talk to him. His guard was down that night; he had recently lost his granddad and his grandma was still upset, and he was convinced, she was not looking after herself. They had always been a devoted couple and she was not coping well without him. That was the night it all started; they had a couple of drinks, then wandered outside. It was a warm night, very still, and the sky had been lit up with stars and a full moon. Before he knew what had hit him, he was rolling around on the grass, his trousers round his ankles, her dress up round her waist, but even he had to admit it was just sex, pure uninhibited sex. From then on, she would book them into a discreet hotel along the coast and then text him and demand he meet her; she never spent the night with him, never had a meal with him, and then one evening after seven months, she arranged to meet him in a different hotel. What she didn't mention to him was that it was actually her wedding anniversary and her husband had booked it for them; he was joining her later, but he had suggested she arrive earlier to have a massage. 'What a massage that turned out to be.' What she didn't know was that her husband had make an extra special effort and had arrived in the room to be met by Simon's backside going up and down with his wife screaming, 'Yes, yes, yes.' All hell broke loose. Mariana was screaming in Italian, and Simon was trying to grab all his clothes and avoid the blows that her husband was aiming at him. He ended up running along the corridor in just his boxer shorts, ironically the ones with the Union Jack on them; her husband had chased after him, throwing his trainers at him as he fled. He had been having nightmares about it ever since. He dreaded bumping into them at any time and always scanned crowds. He didn't know how her husband would react, but he had a feeling he wasn't the first affair she had had. He didn't even know if they were still together. She had tried to phone Simon and had left texts the following day and the week to come.

Simon ignored them all and eventually decided to buy a new SIM card for his phone and changed his number. He knew he was as guilty as her; he had gone into the relationship knowing that she was married, but he could not understand why she had behaved so badly on that afternoon. She had mentioned in one text that her husband should not have surprised her! Simon could see similarities between Mariana and Tania, although Emily had not even hinted that she was the unfaithful type, just spoilt and bored.

Simon turned his mind back to Friday evening. Was it really only two days ago? It had been the eyes, the look of vulnerability and tiredness that he had seen in them, and then the smile, sort of apologetic. He had regretted not following her into the pub; he had seen them go in. He hadn't been able to believe his luck when he had bumped into them on Saturday morning in the harbour. On the first encounter when Emily and Grace were looking over the harbour wall, the wind in her hair, eyes less tired, she looked fresh, her face clear of make-up. She was nothing like Mariana, who would never be seen outside unless she was immaculate. All her clothes had been designer and she spent a fortune on her hair and beauty treatments; this was why he was able to empathise over the way her sister had behaved. They were both first-class bitches.

Emily, he had noticed straight away, wore no wedding ring, and she had been happy to chat to him in a casual, friendly way. He had then been unable to believe his luck when he bumped into her in the cafe. Fate!

He knew he wanted to see more of her. He loved kids; he had three nephews and two nieces, whom he loved to spoil. They were around the same age, all but Freya, who was the most recent and was yet to turn one year old. He suspected that his beautiful niece might have been a slip-up; his sister had always insisted she wanted two children, a boy and girl, which was what she had, and now after an eight-year-gap along popped Freya.

He turned over and checked the time on his mobile phone; it was gone midnight. He had to be up at five in the morning for work; he lay back on his pillow and looked out at the sky through his open window. Was he looking for a new relationship? Was she? Their lifestyles were so different; there was the four-hour travel distance, her father, her children, her job, his job, but he knew that his family would love her and the children. Eventually around one o'clock in the morning, Simon fell asleep.

Monday

Simon had rung Emily about nine thirty the evening before just as she was climbing into her bath accompanied by a glass of wine, and he thanked her for a lovely day out and asked her if she was OK. They had spoken for about twenty minutes, and Simon had suggested that he would like to take them to the seal sanctuary on Tuesday; he explained that he had to work that day. Emily lay in her bed, thinking about the day before; Simon was still interested even after her 'flip' over her sister's treatment of their father. Emily had rung the rest home again when they had got in and was reassured that her father was in bed, watching television. As Emily lay in bed, she became aware of a loud motor noise near her window; it sounded like a lawn mower. Emily stretched and climbed out of bed; drawing back the curtains, she saw George was mowing the lawn in the front of the cottage. As it was only eight thirty, she supposed he was fitting it in before he went to do his shift at the pub. Emily was surprised at how late it was; she was normally such an early riser.

Emily pulled on her tracksuit bottoms and a T-shirt and went downstairs; no sound was coming from either of the children's rooms, and she guessed they would sleep for quite a while longer after their bike ride the day before. Emily reached for the kettle to make herself a cup of coffee; she pulled down a second cup and went to the front door, holding up the cup and a jar of coffee to indicate to George if he would like one too. As she returned to the kitchen, she heard her mobile phone bleep, telling her that she had a text message. She was now keeping the phone on as she had given the rest home her number and told them to only contact her and not bother Tania. Dotty had seemed quite happy to follow this plan. Picking up her phone, she opened her texts: 'hi, hw R U this morning. C u l8t x'. Simon was already texting her. Emily texted back: 'fine, just having a coffee c u l8t 2 x'.

Emily looked around the small lounge whilst she was waiting for the kettle to boil, humming contentedly. It looked much more cheerful now the clean covers were back on the furniture. They really had been quite dirty, and she was glad that she had taken the time last night whilst the children were showering to put them back on. Maybe she would take down the nets and wash the windows. Emily heard the kettle click off; she went through and made herself and George a coffee. She presumed that the three fingers he had held up had indicated three spoons of sugar. There was a tap at the back door. Opening it, she found George standing there with a plug in his hand; he gratefully took the coffee from Emily and asked her if she could plug in his hedge trimmer to enable him to cut the front hedge.

Emily wandered back into the lounge and decided that she would finish off what she had started. Firstly, though, she would check on her father. Emily was happy when she came off the phone; her father seemed to have settled in well. She felt comfortable every time she spoke to whichever member of staff answered the phone. She pulled up a chair and took down the net curtains; straight away, light flooded into the room. Emily put the net into the washing machine along with the one from the kitchen and then filled a bowl with hot soapy water to clean the windows. Half an hour later, Emily stood in the lounge and admired her work; not many people would be willing to come away and clean their accommodation. Most would complain and demand their money back, but Emily found it quite therapeutic. Looking at the clock, she saw it was nearly a quarter to ten; she could hear signs overhead that the children were waking up, and as Emily went through to the stairs, she decided that they would all go to the village for breakfast. She poked her head round each door and told both children what they would be doing, before going into her own room to change. It took the children and Emily only another twenty minutes to be ready, and George assured her he would unplug the electric cable and shut the back door behind him. Emily sensed he could be trusted and was a good friend to Gwen; he seemed to keep a look out for her and was always available to help out.

As they went through their gate, Mary was just coming out of hers. Each greeted the other, Mary adding that she was going to the post office. Emily found herself inviting her for a coffee; after all, it was a repayment for her kind welcome, and it didn't seem that Mary had many visitors. Emily had not seen anyone coming in or out and the old lady had seemed lonely when they had talked on Saturday morning. They all walked down into the village at a slower pace to accommodate Mary. Emily suggested they stop at the old school which was near the post office, as it was a tea room when not being used as a school for the television programme. Mary and Emily found a seat outside in the morning sunshine, which overlooked the harbour, and whilst Emily went inside to order, Mary sat with the children asking them about school and their friends.

Emily carried out a tray with two lattes and two strawberry milkshakes and a large plate with a selection of Danish pastries on it. The children each fell on a large pain aux raisin, and Mary and Emily decided to cut each of the other two into half and share; they both giggled like two conspirators.

Emily and the children spent a happy hour listening to Mary telling them all about the village; she had attended school in the same building they were sitting in. Emily suggested that they went on their way and stopped holding Mary up; she promised that she still intended to have a BBQ on Thursday night, especially as George had now mowed the lawn.

The children asked if they could walk up the hill to the main road and then come down along the coastal path. Emily thought this would be a good idea; the day before had been a full day and that day it would be nice to do something less energetic. As they reached the main road, Emily suggested that they call into the small greengrocers and buy some salad food. Outside on the pavement, Emily and the children selected lettuce, tomatoes, and cucumber; inside, they picked up salad onions, beetroot, Cornish new potatoes, and strawberries. Emily noticed that they were also selling bedding plants twenty-four per tray, two trays for five pounds. Emily decided that she would treat Gwen to a few plants in the empty pots that stood outside the door. Emily missed doing a bit of gardening; every light evening throughout the year, she would spend an hour or so in her garden at home. She always found it helped her to unwind and the fresh air helped her to sleep. She hated the dark winter evenings as it was always dark by the time she got home and the garden was always colourless until the bulbs came out. The owners of the shop offered to drop off the purchases later in the day so that they could continue their walk without the bags; they seemed to know where they were staying.

Emily and the children continued along the main road to the path that would bring them round back into the village and to the cottage. As they looked over the harbour wall, they could see that the lifeboat was out on the slipway; both children wanted to go down and see what was going on. It seemed that the lifeboat station was holding an open day and lots of visitors were milling around. Grace went over to the lifeboat where some of the volunteers were lifting children on to have a look around. Max hung back with another boy around his age; trying to look 'cool', he wandered into the lifeboat station and looked around at the displays. The other boy followed him. 'Hi, I'm Pete. You're staying in Gwen's house, aren't you? I live three doors away. That's my sister talking to yours in the boat.'

Max and Pete struck up a conversation whilst Emily kept her eye on Grace.

When the children got bored, Emily suggested they went back to the cottage for lunch. Pete and his sister, whose name was Mel, followed them. The children chatted as they went up the hill; as they got to the gate, the other children invited Max and Grace round later as they had a big trampoline in their garden. The children rushed down their lunch, eager to get out playing on the trampoline with their new friends. Emily took her cup of tea outside and sat on the front doorstep. The solitary border needed to be weeded; she wondered if there were any tools in the shed. Emily pulled herself to her feet and went to the small shed in the garden and looked for tools. Emily spent a pleasant hour weeding and digging. As she finished, a small van pulled up and the greengrocer got out with a box of her morning purchases. He asked where she would like the box, then placed it on the kitchen work surface, pointing out that his wife had added a small pot of clotted cream for the strawberries, waving away Emily's offer of payment. The plants were placed on the front step, and Emily stayed outside for another half hour, planting them. In the background, Emily could hear the excited squeals and yelps of the children as they played.

'Hello there.' Emily looked up as she recognised Gwen's voice. 'What are you up to?'

Emily got up and opened the gate. 'I hope you don't mind, but I love gardening and the children are playing with the children along the road.' Gwen looked at the fruits of Emily's labour. Emily could see a glint in Gwen's eyes, which she suspected were close to tears.

'It looks beautiful, thank you. I understand from Mary you have been busy in the house. I do apologise I have let things go rather with my mum, and really it's so kind of you to do what you have done.' Gwen sounded sad and tired. 'I need to repay your kindness.'

Emily found herself offering a cup of tea, just as Mary put her head out of her back door. Emily invited Mary to come round, and the three of them spent the next hour sitting in the back garden, drinking tea, eating chocolate biscuits, whilst planning what Gwen needed to have done to do the cottage up and make it more appealing to the letting market. She explained that it wasn't actually making her the living she had intended it to and that she only had a small pension. She agreed that she needed to get the whole cottage painted—both inside and out. It was another job for George, who it turned out seemed to be the local odd job man.

Once both ladies had returned to their own homes, with invitations to come to the BBQ at seven o'clock on Thursday evening, each offering to bring food for the table—Mary was going to bring a pavlova and Gwen was going to make a green salad—Emily returned the cups to the kitchen and decided to go and find the children and have a quick walk before tea. Emily knocked the door and was met by a pretty, petite blonde woman about the same age as herself. 'Hi, I'm Emily, Max and Grace's mum,' she said, holding out her hand.

'Hi, nice to meet you. I'm Sheila. The children have got on like a house on fire. They are in the garden building a den.' Sheila held open the door and indicated to Emily to come in. Sheila led the way into the back garden and called the children.

Emily explained to both her children that she thought they would go for a walk before tea; both asked if Pete and Mel could come. Emily suggested that maybe Sheila would like to join them. Both families set off, Pete and Mel suggesting that they go in the opposite direction from what Emily and the children had previously gone. Sheila and Emily chatted pleasantly. Sheila explained that she was a single mum and worked at the local school. Emily explained that it was a coincidence and explained her situation. Ten minutes later, they came upon a small park with some equipment. The children ran off to use the equipment whilst Sheila and Emily found a seat and sat talking and taking in the view which was stunning; they were looking right across Port Isaac bay towards the coastline, towards Tintagel. After a while, Emily heard her mobile bleep, telling her she had a text: 'hi, where are you? I am in the pub. Would you like to join me?' Simon had obviously just finished work. Emily looked at the time; it was six thirty. 'Wow, I didn't realise the time.' Sheila and Emily both smiled and called the children to them, 'Come along, it's gone teatime.'

Emily texted back to Simon, telling him that they were in the park and had to go home for tea first. 'Here all evening bring the children and come down when you are ready' was the reply. Before they parted, Emily invited Sheila and the children to come to the BBQ. Sheila said she would love to come and promised some potatoes out of her garden and some tomatoes from the greenhouse. Sheila also loved gardening and grew vegetables, salad, and fruit to save on her shopping bill.

Once back at the cottage, Emily asked the children if they wanted to go to the pub. Neither showed much interest that night; they both were tired and quite dirty. Emily suggested that Grace went for a shower before tea and Max could have his after tea. Emily started to prepare the salad, wondering what she should do; she could ask Mary to pop round to be with the children or she could tell Simon that she couldn't come that night and stay at home. Twenty minutes later, both children and Emily sat down for tea. Emily had made a decision and texted Simon, explaining that she wouldn't come down that night as they had had a busy day and were all tired out. After tea, they cleared up, and whilst Max went for a shower Emily sat and read to Grace. By eight thirty, both children were ready for bed. Emily helped a very tired Grace up the stairs, and Max asked her if she minded him going to bed and reading for a while. Downstairs, Emily decided to take a glass of wine outside and sit in the garden for a while, a real self-indulgent treat; she never had time to do things like this or soak in a long bath at home. Just as she sat down, she heard the gate open. Simon appeared round the corner of the bungalow.

Simon was holding up a bottle of wine. 'If the mountain won't go to Mohammed, etc.,' he said with a smile. Emily went in and got a second glass and the bottle opener for Simon.

They sat sipping their wine; at first, there was a bit of a pregnant pause. The conversation was stilted as they started talking about their day. Emily explained that she had made a new friend in Sheila and the children had also made two new friends. Soon though, they found they were talking easily and the time passed quickly; they stayed in the garden until Emily found herself yawning.

Simon stood up to take his leave, asking if she had thought any more about visiting the seal sanctuary the next day. Emily agreed that the children would love to go there, and they arranged to be ready by ten o'clock the following morning. As Emily saw him out of the gate, Simon lent forward and gently brushed his lips to hers. 'Till tomorrow then.' And he was off back down the road, whistling.

Gwen

Gwen sat in her armchair that evening with a plate of cheese and biscuits and a small glass of whisky; it was her preferred tipple of an evening. She was thinking about her earlier discussion with Emily and Mary and what she needed to do to bring the cottage up to a standard that would generate income.

Gwen had lived in Cornwall all her life; as a girl, she had lived in St Austell. She had gone to secretarial college when she left school at fifteen and then gotten a job as a secretary. Not bad for a girl who was brought up in the 1940s by a single parent, who worked as a cleaner to ensure that her daughter had the best life possible that she could give her.

Gwen had met her husband at eighteen, a Cornish lad, the brother of one of her friends. She and Charlie had married the day after her twenty-first birthday; her mother would not give her consent before then, and in those days, you had to be twenty-one before you reached the age of consent.

Gwen was really close to her mum and had learnt to drive as soon as she and Charlie had found a house they could afford just outside St Ives so she could see her mum regularly.

Gwen had grown up without her father, who had never returned from the Second World War. Her mother had never remarried and

Gwen had no brothers or sisters. Her mum had never had any brothers or sisters either. Her mum had eventually lost touch with her dad's family once both his parents had died, so she had been looking forward to Gwen giving her grandchildren.

But it was never meant to be; after ten years of trying, Gwen and Charlie resigned themselves to it never happening. And then one night, Charlie never came home; they found his body two days later. The police said it was a hit and run; the driver was never found. That had been nearly forty-five years ago.

Charlie had had a small life insurance and their mortgage was covered by insurance as well. Gwen had used the money and the sale of the house a couple of years later to move and make a new life for herself; she had found it difficult to drive near where his body had been found. She had also thought, as had the police, that whoever it was that had run Charlie down had been a local. Gwen didn't like the thought that she could pass that person daily. Both Charlie and Gwen loved the area around Port Isaac, and she had been lucky to have found the cottage that she was in now. She had also managed to get a job quickly in the local doctor's surgery. Three years later, she had bought the second cottage to provide a small income along with her wage.

Some people described Gwen as homely; she was a cheery, white-haired countrywoman, a bit overweight, which she always said was because of either her age or slow metabolism and nothing to do with ale and pasties. Others, especially strangers, often mistook her for Stephanie Cole, who thanks to the programme *Doc Martin* being filmed in and around the village was a familiar figure. Stephanie had played Auntie Joan for a few episodes until they killed her off. Gwen was certainly not ready to be killed off, and she occasionally had been known to play on people's mistake to earn herself a free drink or even a meal.

Gwen had retired from the doctor's surgery when it became a necessity for her to travel up and down to see her mum more often, and now at the age of seventy-four, she was still driving and had lots of friends in and around the area. But she was beginning to think that maybe she should consider cutting down on the number of trips she was making to Truro. She had less energy nowadays and her mum's mind wasn't what it had been. The day before had been distressing as her mum hadn't recognised Gwen. She had mistaken Gwen for her own mother, whom Gwen did resemble now. But it was pretty upsetting when she had kept asking where 'my little Gwen' was. At ninety-six, Gwen's mum had always been happy in the rest home. She had been there for the last ten years, but her money was quickly running out, and Gwen knew that before long she would need to contribute to the cost of her mum staying there. Gwen returned to the problem of the cottage; she pulled her pad and pen on to her lap and started to write out a list. Firstly, she would ask George if he could paint the outside for her and maybe the outside of her own cottage, which she had also neglected. Then she would ask him to put the cottage on his list of gardens that he mowed and kept tidy; at least that would give it more kerb appeal, as Emily had suggested. She felt guilty that Emily had felt the need to clean and do the gardening. She had even done the windows and nets along with the covers on the furniture. 'Have I really taken my eye completely off the ball?' Gwen said out loud. Gwen knew the answer to that question, but although it was an excuse, she knew that it was really the time she spent visiting her mum that zapped all her energy.

Gwen moved across to her desk, which was as untidy as the rest of the room; she rummaged around until she found her building society savings book and checked the balance. She calculated that she would need around 2,000 pounds to get both cottages looking at their best, and that would only be the outside. She also knew she needed to advertise the other cottage better and make sure she had a better occupancy rate than she did at present, and she knew exactly the person she needed to ask to help her.

Tuesday

Tuesday morning, day four of the holiday, Emily realised they only had another two days and so far had not been to visit the pixies for Grace, nor had they been to Boscastle and Tintagel for Max, not that either had raised the subject. Emily got up at seven thirty and went downstairs and made a picnic for them all to take with them. She didn't want Simon to feel he had to buy lunch. He seemed very polite, and she suspected he would insist on paying.

Emily had looked up the seal sanctuary on the map; it was down in the south of Cornwall on the Helford Estuary and in a village called Gweek. The advert said that they also had other animals there such as otters, penguins, sheep, ponies, and goats. Occasionally, they had dolphins and turtles too. Emily estimated it would take about an hour to reach the centre; she decided she would suggest that she would drive that day.

At eight thirty, she went up and woke both children and told them where they would be going that day. Grace was excited she would be able to pet some animals. Max was a little less excited but declared it would be cool. He was becoming a teenager, and Emily knew that most of her friends with teenage boys found that they never became excited about anything that their parents suggested; they didn't want to seem 'uncool'. At least, Max still talked to her rather than grunts; she guessed this was still to come. She did what she had done for the last two mornings and rang the rest home where her father was. That day, she spoke to Dotty again, who informed her that he would be going out on a trip to a local attraction called 'Compton Acre'; she explained that the residents liked to be pushed round the gardens, looking at the ponds and plants, and then having a cup of tea and a cake in the tea rooms. She told Emily that he had played bingo the night before and had won a box of chocolates, which he had shared with the other residents and the staff. She told Emily that he was already making friends and the residents and staff all liked him. Emily was content when she came off the phone; she still intended to take her father home on Friday afternoon, but she was glad he was enjoying his little 'holiday'.

Emily also quickly texted Wendy to check on Bruno and Marie to give her an update.

When Simon knocked the door, they were all ready. He was prompt. Emily wondered if this had more to do with the constant tight schedules of his job rather than wanting to see her, but Emily hoped that it might be the latter. Emily suggested she drove, but Simon had the use of a people carrier from work and declared that it would be more comfortable. As Emily had estimated, it took just over an hour to reach the village and the signposts were good; they never got lost once.

They spent a pleasant four hours at the sanctuary, listening to talks about the seals and how they started the business and what the aims were; they picnicked in the grounds, then each of the children purchased a gift from the shop with their holiday money. They had taken lots of photos to show their friends when they got home.

Simon had asked the children during the day where they would like to visit and if they had made any plans, then he had listened to both their ideas.

On the way back, Emily noticed they were not going the same way as they had come. After about twenty minutes, Simon turned off the main road. When she asked where they were going, all he did was wink.

Suddenly, Emily saw the sign, 'Pixie land'. Simon drew the car up in front of a gate that had wooden toadstools and pixies outside. Grace became excited as she looked through the window, climbing over Max in her eagerness to get out of the car. The four of them spent a good hour walking round the garden, following the 'treasure' hunt map that they purchased while buying their entrance tickets; all the proceeds would go to the local hospice. Grace especially enjoyed running through the pathways and finding the next clue. Max entered into the spirit of things to encourage her enjoyment.

Emily noticed a conspiratorial whispering between Simon and Max at one stage; she smiled to herself, pleased at how well both her children got on with Simon. As the got back to the car, Emily saw Simon wink at Max as she paid for the little pixie figurine that Grace wanted to buy at the small wooden shed that stood by the gate.

'What are you two up to?' Emily questioned as they all climbed into the car.

'Nothing,' both replied in unison.

Twenty minutes later when Simon once again took a detour off the main road, Emily could see what they had been up to; in front of them was a McDonald's. Simon wrapped his arm around her shoulders. 'He was a good sport to go along with Grace's wishes. I would have hated it if my sister had wanted to go there as a child,' Simon explained. This was a rare treat for both children as Emily liked them to eat healthy, and also, it would be late for Grace by the time they got back to the cottage. Emily actually found herself enjoying their meal; it was a treat for all of them as Simon couldn't remember the last time he had had a McDonald's either.

It was nearly eight o'clock, and Grace had been falling asleep in the last ten minutes in the car. Both children had thanked Simon for taking them out and had talked about their favourite parts of the day all the way home. Simon had won them over, and Emily knew he was well on the way to winning her over as well.

Emily decided to invite Simon in when they pulled up outside the cottage. Both children ran ahead to open the door whilst Emily and Simon brought in the bags from the car. Emily sent the children upstairs to get ready for bed and put the kettle on for a cup of coffee. Simon had agreed to have a quick one. He needed to get back as he was due to be on the set at eleven o'clock; they were filming a night scene. Emily took both cups of coffee into the lounge and placed them on the table. She was aware of Simon standing behind her; she turned slowly and found herself drifting into his arms. They stood for a few minutes, looking at each other. Slowly, as if in a film, Emily found them moving closer together, their lips touching softly at first and then more hungrily. Emily gave herself up to his embrace. She could not believe how passionate the feelings coursing through her had become. Both of them suddenly became aware of footsteps on the stairs and broke away in time before Max came through the door. Emily was not sure how the children would react if they found Simon to be more than a friend.

'Simon, are you coming to our BBQ on Thursday night? Mum has invited Mary and Gwen, and Sheila, Pete, and Max are coming. They are all bringing things.' He stopped suddenly and looked at his mother.

'It's OK, isn't it?' he enquired as though he had noticed a slight atmosphere that he couldn't understand.

'Yes, of course, it's OK. I just haven't got round to asking yet, but Simon, you will come, won't you?' Emily turned to Simon.

Emily suddenly realised that George was missing from her guest list; she made a mental note to ask him in the morning.

'Love to. Sounds as if I will need to go shopping though. How about I ask George for a couple of bottles of wine?' Simon smiled at Max and roughed his hair. 'And some bottles of coke for you lot.'

Emily and Simon drank their coffee whilst Max watched a programme he liked on TV; at nine o'clock, Simon took his leave.

Emily walked him to the gate; that night they were more aware of their feelings towards each other while saying goodbye. Each was a little uneasy as if a line had been stepped over and there was no going back.

Emily gently touched Simon's cheek; suddenly they were both in a warm embrace, kissing each other as if they had been lovers for weeks rather than having only known each other for four days. Emily did not want the kiss to end.

Later as she was climbing into bed, she had a text from Simon: 'nite nite, its bloody cold out here on the moor there's a mist not sure if it's romantic or sinister'.

Emily texted back: 'nite nite xx'. She would have liked to have added more and suggested that she could warm him up, that it could be romantic if they were together on the moor, but she didn't want to rush things. She still didn't really know how she felt; up till now all her romances had been done away from the children, not in front of them. She closed her eyes and fell asleep to the memory of those stolen kisses.

Mary's Story

Mary sat at her lounge window, which she did most evenings. Mary preferred listening to the radio to watching the TV, especially on summer nights when people were out and about and the warm air came through the window.

She saw Simon leaving and smiled to herself as she saw the beginning of a new romance, and it started her on her reminiscing.

Originally by birth, Mary was from the East End of London, but she thought of herself as a true Cornwall resident. She could no longer remember her home in London or the family she had left behind. Mary had been the eldest of six children although she had never seen the last baby; he had been born after Mary and her sister had left, and she had been told about him in a letter that her mum had sent, not that her mum could read and write, but she had managed to get a lady from their local Red Cross to draft a letter for her.

Mary and her sister Martha had been sent away at the start of the Second World War as evacuees. Mary could still remember the feeling of bewilderment she felt when her mum had said goodbye to them both one morning, and her dad had walked them to the train station at Waterloo. They had both initially presumed that they were going on a trip. Once at the station, they found it was full of parents and children of all ages. Some children were crying; others were pleading with their parents to go home. Mary and Martha soon realised that this was a trip with a difference. Their father had taken them to a desk and given their names, and they had been given tags, then their father had said goodbye and walked off. That was the last time either girl had seen their birth family.

Mary and Martha had sat on the train, quietly holding each other's hands, hoping above hope that they would not be separated. At one stage, they had all disembarked from the train and names had been called out. They had been herded into another train. It had been hours before they had steamed into their final destination of Exeter.

Mary and Martha had been two lucky ones in all respects. Jim and Pearl had been a lovely couple, with a son, Jimbo, who was three years older than Mary. Mary and Martha had had a good life with them and they had been fantastic parents. Pearl had been unfortunate and had lost children before she had Jimbo and never had any more afterwards, so they offered their large family farm house to children who were being evacuated. Mary and Martha never saw their birth parents or siblings again, although Mary was now in touch with her only surviving brother, Sid, who lived in Brighton. The Blitz had flattened the family home and taken all but Sid with them. Sid had been out with his mates at the time of the start of the raid and had been down in the underground. When he came up the following morning, he had found devastation. The day Mary found out what had happened was the only time in her life that she had ever sworn, and by today's standard, running across the farmyard, shouting 'bloody Hitler' was mild, but that was the influence that Pearl and Jim had on both girls—gentle, churchgoing, law-abiding, hard-working salt-of-the-earth couple. Jimbo had been of similar nature to his father. Mary wiped a tear from her eye with the back of her hand. She tried not to think about the life she had had on the farm. Both she and Martha had always thought of them all as one big happy family, and after about five years, she had started to call Jim and Pearl Dad and Mum. Mary and Martha had been adopted by Jim and Pearl once the authorities had established that the surviving family of aunts and uncles would be unable to have them to live with them. Pearl had always tried to keep the girls in touch with their roots and had framed the three small photos their mother had packed for them on that day. Mary now had two that stood on her mantelpiece, and she guessed Martha still had the other one.

Mary had taken to country life better than Martha, who had moved to Plymouth once she had been old enough to leave; she had phoned and visited but could never embrace the life that Mary had. Mary had stayed at home. Life had not been entirely rosy. Mary and Martha had always been well fed and well treated and knew they were loved. Holidays had been great—long days spent outside, running through the meadows, helping with the harvest, picnicking down by the stream that ran through the woods that were part of the farm. Further afield, on bicycle rides with other local children, they would go fishing in the local river or swimming in a local pond. Harvest always held fond memories for Mary of helping to pack up large picnics that they carried up to the fields along with flagons of cider—all of them sitting down together and the farm hands demolishing the baskets in what seemed like minutes.

But all that changed just before her thirteenth birthday when a tragic accident killed Jimbo. By then, Jimbo was working alongside their father on the farm, and he knew that one day he would take over and be the farmer whilst his dad and mum took a back seat; he had always dreamed of raising a family of his own and had talked about building a small bungalow for the parents. He had even picked out a plot for them. That was never to be. Neither parents properly recovered from that tragedy. The farm was sold and they had all moved to a bungalow with a large garden near Port Isaac. The only reminder of their previous farm roots had been four chickens and two old ducks. Pearl had died three years later; the hospital called it heart failure, but Mary knew it had been a broken heart. After Mary and Martha had got married, Jim went fishing one day and never returned. Again, Mary had known that he could not face life on his own.

Mary had been nineteen when she married and Martha had married two years later at seventeen. When Mary married Bert in a small ceremony at the local church where Pearl was buried, they had bought the bungalow. Bert had worked at the Delebore Slate mine. He had played darts in the local social club, read the lesson each week in church, and then come home and given her and the four children a thrashing. The first time he had hit Mary he had sworn it was an accident and that it would never happen again, but whenever he had taken a drink, he would find some fault and then hit out.

Mary had had four children in five years, two boys and two girls— boy, girl, boy, girl. Mary had called the children Fredrick (Fred for short) and Edith after her birth parents and Jim and Pearl after her adopted parents. Bert wasn't interested in the names of the children. The children lived in fear of their father. Mary had constantly found herself making excuses at school and the health visitor for their bruises. She had blamed it on clumsiness, boisterousness, bad behaviour. As the boys got older, the situation got worse as they argued back with their father. The girls wanted to experiment with make-up and fashion and they would also argue. In some ways, it had been a relief when she got a knock at the door to say that Bert had been injured and was in hospital. The works had sent a car to take her straight to the hospital, but they had been unable to save him; he had had terrible crush injuries.

The children had been more upset than she had imagined them to be, and as they grew older, she had found it hard to cope with them. A mother on her own with four teenage children was not easy. Martha on the other hand had married well and had two lovely girls, with a big house and a lovely man. She had always seen her sister regularly, but she had never known how abusive Mary's life had been. Mary was close to her nieces and her great-nieces and great-nephews. They all visited her still, living in and around the Plymouth area to be near their own parents, whereas Mary's children were scattered around the country and world. Fred had moved to North Yorkshire and was married with three boys. Edith had moved to Canada, where she had married and had two children, and apart from the obligatory Christmas, birthday, and Mother's Day cards and the yearly school photo Mary had never met the family. Edith had died four years ago due to breast cancer, and she had been buried before Mary had been told about her death. Jim had gone into the army; he had been married to army life and occasionally came home to see her, but he had preferred to stay in Cyprus when he came out of the army. Pearl lived in Brighton, which was a coincidence as that was where Sid lived, but Mary had only ever visited her three times, although she used to come down each year with her four children. But now that they were all grown-up and had left home, Pearl found it hard to get around as she had arthritis. Mary had not seen her for nearly five years.

The children didn't even keep in touch with each other; she wrote regularly to each of the three surviving children, and it was she who told them what the other was doing. She definitely wrote more letters to her children than they did to her.

Wednesday

Wednesday arrived with a thick mist that promised to lift and reveal a nice, sunny day. Max had asked the night before when they would be able to go to Boscastle and Tintagel Castle. Emily decided that that day would be a good day; the next day was their last day, and she planned to have the BBQ the next night. She had no idea what Simon was up to that day; it would probably depend on how long he had to work the night before.

Emily went downstairs to make a coffee; looking at her watch, she saw that it was seven thirty. She decided that she should put on some washing before the children got up. She didn't want to take bags of dirty washing home for the weekend, when there was a washing machine available in the cottage and the weather was good for drying. Emily liked order; she knew she would be rushing around all day Saturday. Emily knew that Saturday would be taken up with picking up her dad, the dog, and eventually having to speak to her sister. Although Emily was much calmer, she still could not believe that Tania had been so selfish. She loaded up the washing machine, slammed the door, and turned it on; she stood looking out of the kitchen window, deep in thought. How was it that Tania could be so selfish? Why did she expect everything and everybody to revolve around her? Life for Tania was all about her creature comforts. Emily had been horrified when Maria had explained

Tania's behaviour to her. How did a mother justify letting her young son look after his own grandfather whilst she lay in bed? Tania was quite capable of looking after her own father for a week. Also, Wendy had explained her view of the situation, and on reflection, Emily had concluded that maybe her dad was safer and even happier in the home than being looked after by his elder daughter. 'Well,' Emily thought, 'never again will I ever ask Tania for any help whatsoever.' The washing machine made a noise and brought her back into the real world; she took a sip of her coffee and realised that she must have been standing dreaming for a while as the coffee was now cold. Tipping it down the sink, she re-boiled the kettle and made a second cup just as a text came through on her mobile:

'Hi bbe'

'Hi u'

'Wuu2 2day?'

'Takin kids 2 Boscastle an Tintagel'

'can i cum wit u?'

'Only if I drive'

'k wat time'

'Leavin @ 10.30'

'C u in 2 hrs cnt w8'

'c u soon me 2 xx'

Emily put her phone down and grabbed the map; she wanted to make sure that she knew her way now that she had suggested driving. Taking a piece of paper, she jotted down the route. Turning to the guide part of the map, she read:

To really appreciate the beauty of Boscastle, take a short walk . . .
The right hand harbour footpath takes you seaward to stunning
viewpoints. You can continue onwards to Pentargon Waterfall,
featured in Hardy's novel 'A Pair of Blue Eyes'.

That sounded like a good idea—a nice coastal walk if the mist cleared. She remembered going to Tintagel when she was little and recalled that there were a lot of steps. She decided they would do Boscastle this morning and if they had time Tintagel in the afternoon and maybe a cream tea; she seemed to remember a little teashop in a corner where her mum and she had had a cream tea a few years ago whilst her dad had taken the children off somewhere. Those had been lovely days. Emily had loved holidaying with her parents; she had very fond memories of their camping trips and she was glad that both her children had been able to have such a positive relationship with their grandparents after the breakup of her marriage—simple, quiet, and fun. She was hoping to recapture this atmosphere this week for the children.

Emily laid the table with cereal and fruit juice and put some toast in the toaster ready, then she went upstairs to wake both the children and to get changed herself. As she was dressing, she started to feel sad and wondered whether at the end of the week it would not only be bye-bye Cornwall but also bye-bye Simon. She felt so comfortable and right when they were together, and most importantly for her, he seemed to like and enjoy the company of the children as well.

Once the breakfast was eaten and cleared away, she directed both the children in getting together a picnic whilst she hung out the washing; she also made a mental note that she would need to make a shopping list for the next day's BBQ, which was growing in numbers by the day. There was a knock at the door; expecting it to be Simon, Emily flung open the door, but instead George stood there. 'Just thought I would finish your back garden. I hear you're having a BBQ.'

Emily laughed, 'I was just thinking about that. Would you like to come?'

George gave her a big smile. 'So glad you asked. Taken the liberty of bringing me BBQ grill on the van, it's gas. None of that faffing about with coals and all that cleaning up. I'll ask chef for some sausages and some large prawns as me contribution.' George hung around for a few minutes, explaining that Gwen had phoned him first thing that morning and asked him to take on the garden and whether he could paint the house, but he explained that although he was happy to do odd jobs and his gardens, the painting of the cottage was too big a job and he was going to find someone else to do it for her, someone who was reliable.

Emily had returned to the kitchen to finish packing the picnic when she heard voices; both children came running in. 'Simon's here. He's helping George with the BBQ.'

Emily checked whether George would require electricity before she locked up. They climbed into Emily's car, and she noticed the mist was lifting; the sun was starting to creep through the mist, and it looked like a promising day. Emily remembered that her mum always used to insist that if the day started misty, then it usually meant that a nice day followed.

Emily found her way to Boscastle with no trouble; she was a confident driver and loved negotiating the narrow Cornish lanes. Emily parked the car in the main car park; there didn't seem to be many people around yet, but she was sure that it would soon fill up.

Together, the four of them strolled along down into the harbour. They stopped in front of the national trust shop; Simon suggested that they go in and take a look inside. Simon steered them to a central bank of televisions which were running the story of the floods that had happened in August 2004; both the children stood mesmerised in front of the screens as the story of that fateful day was told. Simon pointed out through the window the way they had just come and explained this had been the path of all the water.

Both children wanted to wander around the shop. They both still had some of their holiday spending money left and wanted to buy presents for their friends. Grace chose quickly and decided to take each of her friends back a pencil, whilst Max, being older, decided that pencils were boring and babyish and wanted something more grown-up, but what?

Grace started to become fidgety. 'Come on, Max. This is boring.' She started picking up and putting down items on display. Emily could feel the lady at the till staring at her.

'Grace, leave things alone.'

'But I am bored. Max is taking so long.'

Simon intervened, 'Hey, why don't you two go into the cafe and get some refreshments before our walk and Max and I will sort out here?'

Emily gave Simon a grateful look. 'Great idea. Coffee?'

'Cappuccino, please.'

Emily and Grace went and found a table and purchased the drinks and a cake each. The cafe was filling up. Emily noticed that a lot of people were dressed for serious walking and wondered if the children or even herself or Simon would find the walk difficult. The map had said it was nearly two miles along the coastal path to the waterfall. Within a few minutes, Simon and Max appeared: Max looked extremely pleased with himself. 'Pencils are for kids.' He looked straight at Grace. 'I've bought rulers.' He brandished one triumphantly.

'Oh, dear,' signed Emily, 'today looks like fun.'

Simon raised his eyebrows. 'That's right, kids.' He looked from one to the other. 'We are going to have fun.' He winked at Emily, showing her that he had deliberately misinterpreted the meaning of what she had said, but both children were already discussing their walk.

Emily glanced across at Simon and winked back.

'I saw that,' Grace said in an exaggerated tone of voice. Simon then winked at her. Grace giggled, and Emily started to relax; the atmosphere was once more jovial and neither of the children was bickering any more. Emily knew that on the whole both of her children got on really well and seldom did bicker, but like all children they had their moments.

Once they had had their drinks, used the loo, and packed their purchases in the children's rucksacks, they set off along the path that followed the contours of the inlet till it reached the harbour and then the sea. The tide was in and the waves slapped against the rocks; the herring gulls screeched overhead and the sun shone. You could taste and smell the salt in the air; it smelt clean and fresh.

Simon pointed out a small blowhole to the children, something that Emily knew she would probably have missed if she had been on her own. Simon took time to explain it to both children who listened, hanging on to his every word.

Before they ascended the cliff path, Simon explained to both children the dangers of walking along a cliff and the importance of following the path and staying in between himself and Emily. Emily felt more relaxed than she had in months; it was so nice for someone else to look after her and the children for once.

They followed the path skywards, stopping now and again to glance down at Boscastle, which was getting smaller, but the view more panoramic. High on the opposite cliff, they could see people walking up to a small building perched on the end of the cliff. 'We've used that in filming.' Simon pointed across the harbour.

'Cor.' Grace was impressed. 'Can we go there?'

'Well, I don't think so, not today. You will be very tired when we get back.' Simon glanced at Emily to check if she was happy with this.

'Yes, especially if we go on to Tintagel so that we can have a cream tea after we have been up the castle ruins,' Emily reminded both children of their plans.

'Oh, yes, please.' Grace rubbed her stomach in an elaborate gesture of being hungry; she was happy again. It didn't take a lot to please either of the children, and Emily cherished every moment; they were both growing up so fast.

Once they reached the top of the path, Emily stood still and exhaled. 'Wow! What a magnificent view!' Simon stood beside her, a hand on each of the children's shoulders in a protective gesture. Anyone walking past would have assumed they were a happy family on holiday. It felt so right and both Emily and Simon felt this, but neither was confident to voice their feelings yet. Emily dug around for her camera and started snapping.

'Whoa, you need to change the setting.' Emily looked blank. Simon took the camera from her and showed her how to change the setting so she could take a photo of the whole panoramic view in one.

'Oh dear, I never knew it did that.' Emily sounded embarrassed.

'Insider information, one of the camera men showed me last year.' Simon shrugged, changing the subject. 'Do you know I have never been up this side of Boscastle?'

'Nor have I,' replied Emily. 'Look what we have been missing.'

Simon moved forward so that the children were once again between himself and Emily, and they went through the gate on to the cliff path. Simon constantly pointed out plants, birds, and other wildlife. It was obvious that he knew more about the Cornish coast than she would have been able to tell the children about.

It took the little group nearly an hour to walk along the cliff path to the waterfall. They stopped halfway along the path where there was a bench set into the wall that bordered the fields on their right, and everyone had a piece of fruit that Emily had packed. Whilst they sat looking out to see, they enjoyed the warm sunshine.

The waterfall was just as amazing as described in the brochure; it sprung out of the cliff and cascaded down into the sea.

The children were awestruck and stood listening to the noise. Two walkers came up towards them. 'You're seeing her at her best,' said the man. 'All that rain we have had has given her lots of energy.'

The couple stood talking to both Simon and Emily for a few minutes, pointing out the path that would take them down into the little bay and then explaining that they could do a round route to Boscastle, using some of the roads and farmers' fields.

Emily thanked the couple as they moved past them and followed the route that Emily and Simon as well as the children had just walked.

Simon led the way down the path into the small sandy bay; because the cliffs rose up high on each side of the bay, it was warm. Emily spread out a rug on the sand that she had brought and started to empty out the rolls, fruit, and crisps along with bottles of water.

Simon flopped down on his knees beside her; he had also brought bits for the picnic, smiling apologetically. 'Sorry, it's supermarket finest.' He added cocktail sausages, small savoury eggs, along with strawberries and then doughnuts.

Simon, Emily, and the children spent a leisurely hour sitting in the bay until they noticed the tide starting to inch up the beach.

Simon stood up. 'Come on, folks. Think it's time for us to move.' They cleared up in unison, putting the rubbish in the bags, and then started to walk back the way that the couple had earlier suggested. Simon slipped his arm across Emily's shoulder, and she leant closer; they all walked on, comfortable in each other's company.

'Mummy, Mummy, are we going to Tintagel still? Are we going to climb up to the castle?'

'Shall we wait and see when we get there? You might be tired and it's now getting late. Maybe we need to keep it for another holiday, but we still can have our cream tea.' Emily knew she needed to offer a positive choice.

They enjoyed a pleasant walk back to the harbour across fields and down narrow lanes, singing songs that they all knew and a few that Emily didn't; she wasn't into the current pop songs, but Simon and Max seemed to know them all.

By the time they reached the car park, both the children started to get irritable again with each other, a sure sign that Grace was beginning to get tired. Emily steered Grace to the car. 'Come on, let's find that cream tea.'

Emily pointed the car in the direction of Tintagel, and within a short time, they were pulling into the car park. They found a little tea room, not the one that Emily could remember, but it had a good array of cakes and more importantly scones.

Simon ordered three cream teas. Emily had suggested that four might be too much after the picnic. Both the children asked for cola, and for once Emily didn't mind.

It was nearly six o'clock when they piled back into the car for the drive back to Port Isaac. It took just over half an hour, but by the time they pulled up outside the gate, Grace was sound asleep. Simon suggested he carry her inside; he lifted her out of the seat tenderly and followed Emily up the path and through the front door.

'I think she can go straight to bed tonight. I will put her in the shower tomorrow.' Emily led the way up the stairs to the bedroom at the back that Grace occupied, and Simon gently laid her on the bed.

'I'll put the kettle on whilst you sort her out.' Simon backed out of the room. 'Shall I suggest to Max that he grabs his shower?'

'Please,' Emily whispered.

Ten minutes later, Emily and Simon were sitting together in the back garden sipping tea, and Emily was admiring the difference to the garden because of George's labour. It was a pretty little garden, a bit longer than her own garden back in Ringwood.

Max appeared at the back door with wet hair and a cup in his hand. 'I have opened the new milk, Mum.' Emily had a rule in her house: If you opened it, you either told her about it or you could write it on the shopping list, Max was able to do this now with competence, but Grace still needed help.

'Thanks, darling, we will add it to the list for tomorrow.' Emily smiled at her son.

By nine o'clock, they were all tired. Max said good night and went up to his room to read for half an hour before he went to sleep. Emily and Simon moved inside, and Emily opened the fridge and held up a bottle of wine.

'OK, only one. I have to work first thing.'

Emily poured them each a glass, and they took them into the lounge and sat down on the sofa.

Simon set his own glass down on the table and removed her glass from her hand and placed it beside his own, then he turned to Emily; gently, he ran his thumb under her chin and traced the line, slowly cupping it in his hand and pulling her towards him. Emily surrendered her lips to his. She could taste wine and tea on his lips; he took sugar which she didn't, and they tasted sweet. Emily's arms closed around Simon's back, her hands running through his hair as she sank into his kisses.

Slowly, they both fell backwards on to the sofa, still embracing urgently. Simon's hands worked their way up under her T-shirt, tracing the curve of her spine. Her bra was no barrier, and he expertly unclasped it with one hand, cupping her breast with the other. As he started to tease at her nipple, Emily let out a moan. Swiftly, Simon lifted her T-shirt above her head and sank his lips over her nipple, whilst gently moulding her other breast with his fingers, tweaking her nipple as he gently bit the other one. Emily moaned more; it was so long since she had felt like this.

The only light in the room was the light that shone from the street light outside, casting an orange glow into the room.

Emily became aware that Simon's hand had moved lower and was moving slowly along the hem of her shorts. She could feel his arousal pressing against her thigh, straining to escape. He slowly started to undo the zip on her shorts; tentatively, she reached down and started to undo his jeans. Both were starting to breathe heavily. Emily knew that she should stop, but she also knew that she couldn't stop now even if she wanted to; she had not gone this far with another man since she had split up with her ex-husband. She shuddered suddenly at the thought.

'You OK?' Simon stopped. Emily nodded, unable to speak.

Slowly, they sank down on to the floor, shedding the rest of their clothes, and Emily gave herself up to Simon's love making. Slowly and sensitively at first, he sought to please her as well as himself. But they soon were both urgently reaching for a crescendo together.

Slowly, their breathing returned to normal as they lay locked together. Emily was surprised at her own reaction to Simon's touch, and then reality brought her back down to earth. 'Simon, we didn't take any precautions. I don't take the pill.' Emily expected him to tense and react in a negative way.

'It's fate,' he murmured into her hair, and he started to nuzzle into her neck again, pulling her on top of him.

'Fate it might have been, but we can't be stupid,' Emily murmured. 'Please, Simon, let's not be silly.' But even Emily knew she didn't sound convincing.

Simon rolled towards her, reaching out and lifting her back on to him. 'I will sort it tomorrow, if you want me to.' He started again to trace the outline of her breast in a figure of eight movement; Emily found her body reacting over her brain. She arched her back and could feel his manhood poking gently against the inside of her thigh again.

'I want you too.' They started to move in unison once again.

Later lying in her bed on her own, she wondered if this was a holiday romance. Would it end on Friday along with her break? She was also scared that she might go home with more than memories.

Just as she was drifting off to sleep, her phone bleeped: 'nite, nite xx'. Emily texted back: 'sweet dreams xx'; another came straight back: 'U bet xx'. Emily smiled and drifted off to sleep.

Simon

When Simon left Emily's holiday home, he felt slightly troubled. Neither of them had been prepared for the way the day had ended. Did he regret it? 'No,' he said out loud. What he felt for Emily and her kids wasn't something he had felt before. What he did know was that he wanted to carry on seeing them all when she left to go home.

He hadn't mentioned it yet to Emily, but his contract ran out at the end of June. They were running a bit behind schedule, but the company wanted the filming wrapped up before the summer got underway. He had applied for a few new jobs and had two offers at the moment; the first was a documentary about Cornish smugglers. The second was in Scotland. Simon had been thinking that a change of scene would be a good idea, but now as long as Emily wanted to continue with their relationship it was the Cornish smugglers who would win. He still had a week to let them know.

Simon arrived home and sat for the second time in a week looking at the house; for the first time in ages, he really looked at where he lived. It was a tip, to be honest, a lad's pad; anyone driving past would automatically think that it was a bunch of 'surf bums' who lived there, and they would be right. It was technically true; none of the lads ever tidied up. It was straight in from work and out to play. The surfboards and wetsuits cluttered up the porch.

Simon had money in the bank, some from the nest egg his grandparents had left and more that he had added over the last three years. He had enough to put down a large deposit on a house.

He sat listening to the waves in the distance, dreaming of himself, Emily, and the children all living together as a family.

'Whoa, mate,' he found himself talking out loud again. He didn't even know if she wanted a relationship. This might be a holiday romance; he might have read her wrongly. But then surely someone looking for a holiday romance would have been prepared for all eventualities. Tonight had certainly seemed on the spur of the moment. It had been for him; all week he had been telling himself, 'Slowly, slowly.'

Before getting out of his van, Simon texted 'nite, nite xx'; before he could open the front door, a text bounced back: 'sweet dreams xx'.

Well, at least she wasn't regretting what had happened; he sent another text: 'U bet xx'.

He would be more prepared the next evening, just in case.

George

George William George was born in September 1949. George had always had to explain his stupid name, but his mother had reasoned that as his father—who was an army captain—always called boys and men by their surname it would be less intimidating to have the same first name and last name. But his father had managed to intimidate him all his life.

It still didn't work even at sixty-three, and even though his father was now eighty-nine, he still felt that he was in trouble every time his father spoke to him. As a child, he would do anything he would to please his father, but one word 'George' sent terror through his veins. As a small child, his mother had done all she could to protect him and Kim, his sister. They had minimal contact with him. His father had never shown any preference for either himself or Kim. Both were expected to be perfect individuals, exceed at school, go to college and then university, and never get into trouble.

George's mother had died years ago; at the time, George who had followed his father into the army was posted in Northern Ireland. Neither parent had mentioned how ill his Mother was—not to him or to his sister Kim, who was travelling in Australia at the time. It had come as a terrific shock to him, when the company chaplain had called him into his office and given him the news that his mother had died.

Kim had never forgiven their father; she had flown home for the funeral with a small suitcase and two days' clothes. The day after the funeral, she had gone into Aldershot and bought a large suitcase, packed up all the things she wanted to take with her, and had not exchanged one word with their father. She had returned to her boyfriend in Australia, moved on to his sheep farm, married, had three children in three years, and had never returned to England. This had left George at the mercy of his father's temper. George had gone out once to Australia, just after his marriage had broken up, but he and his brother-in-law had not had anything in common and did not really hit it off. Kim and George found they also didn't have much in common any longer, and George had been glad when his two weeks were up and they were back to sending Christmas cards and a brief note. Now it was George who had to be on call for his father; although he had managed to get him into sheltered housing, he still got demands to hot tail it to Aldershot to fix something or sort out a problem, often caused by his father in the first place.

One of the reasons that George got on so well with Gwen was that they were both looking after their elderly parents and were able to share their woes together.

George had always known that it was expected of him to go into the army. He had joined up as soon as he was of age, but he had never really liked the life. He had seen more in the fifteen years that he was in there than most men saw in a lifetime and worse. He never talked about his time in the army; he had never discussed his tours of duty with his wife when he was home, and she had cited this as part of the problem when she had petitioned for divorce. The fact that she had had numerous affairs whilst he was away resulting in her becoming pregnant by another man was not part of the problem according to her lawyers.

George had only been dating Amanda for a couple of months when he had found out about his mother and had come home. She had been so sympathetic, so understanding, always there to listen; before his compassionate leave was up, he had proposed and they were engaged to be married on his next leave.

They had married in Aldershot, and the only members of his family present had been his auntie and his grandparents on his mother's side and a handful of army mates, who were probably there for the free food and booze rather than the wedding ceremony. His father had refused to attend; he hadn't liked Amanda and had all but forbidden George to marry. If he had not been over the age of twenty-one, then he would have stopped it for sure, but George had ignored his father, who to this day had always reminded him that he had been correct. George and Amanda had had three children quickly, one for each leave, but on the whole he had been an absent father, leaving all the upbringing of the children to Amanda. And although she had her parents close by, she had all the responsibility, not unusual for an army family. George had been away for each of the children's births and had never had a bond with them.

Amanda had liked a social life; she enjoyed the dances and discotheques that Aldershot had offered in the 1970s. It hadn't been until she became pregnant for the fourth time whilst he was away that George realised that people had known about her affairs. He had felt that everyone was laughing at him behind his back. Slowly, he had slipped into depression and threw himself into his job.

George had remained in the army until he was thirty-three and then decided to cut his losses; he was estranged from his children, his sister was in Australia, and unless he had to, he didn't make much contact with his father. There was no reason for George to remain doing what he was doing; he had given fifteen years to the army by then and wanted and needed a complete rest.

George had taken what money he had and upped sticks and moved to the North Cornish coast. Here he had managed to buy a small run-down fisherman's cottage. The previous owners had been elderly and had let the place to go to ruin nearly. He had worked tirelessly over the years to get it up together and was really proud of his small abode.

He had taken on small odd jobs to keep himself in food and basics and to fund the renovation work. His present job at the pub meant he got a main meal every day when he worked; one thing he had found out was that his cooking wasn't up to much.

George knew he was a popular member of the community; most of the locals accepted him now as one of their own. He was always jovial and ready to help out wherever he could, but what no one, not even Gwen knew, was that his trips to the doctor were not for his back. He visited the doctor to get antidepressants and sleeping tablets. He had been suicidal on his arrival in Port Isaac. His last tour of duty in the Middle East had been the bloodiest he had ever known and he had lost three of his closest mates. On top of this, he found it hard that he never saw his children at all. Amanda had claimed in the divorce that he had been violent to her and the children, so any contact had to be supervised; the fact that he had never laid a finger on any of them was dismissed. He was in the army, trained to kill. 'He had to be violent, didn't he?' was the line her lawyers took. George hadn't seen this coming and had lost his temper in the court room, which had not helped his case.

He wasn't even sure if his youngest child was his. Amanda had refused DNA testing. He had had to support all three of the children until they were eighteen, even though he never saw them.

His eldest was married and was a successful banker but had not even invited George to his wedding, nor had he let George know when either of his children had been born.

Becca, the middle one, was now thirty-six and lived and worked in Plymouth; she had been in touch since she had left college at twenty. When she had returned home and explained her sexual preference was women her mother had kicked her out of the home. Becca had sought out her father for support and had moved down to live with him in his little cottage for a year before getting a job in Truro and then setting up home with her partner in Plymouth, where they had two children. George idolised his two grandchildren and was able to lavish on to them the love he had not been able to do to his own children. They tried to see each other at least once a month.

The youngest child, from what Becca told him, was an unmarried mother of two and didn't know who the father was. Apparently, Amanda had kicked her out of her home and did not see anything of her, but she didn't want any contact with her father either. Amanda had been spiteful; she had convinced the children that he had been a bad husband and a bad father. Eventually, what she told them sunk in and they believed what she told them.

The only person who knew much about his previous life was Gwen. She had helped out when Becca moved in as she was confused and very upset with her mother's attitude. Gwen had been a motherly figure and supported both of them through a very trying time. Becca was very fond of Gwen and had invited her to be godmother to both the children.

The BBQ

Emily woke early on Thursday morning; she was feeling a mixture of emotions. Had she done the wrong thing last night? Would Simon want to continue with their relationship after Friday? Did she? 'Yes, definitely.' She knew that much.

Glancing at the clock, she saw it was only 5.30 a.m., but she decided to get up and go down and make a cup of tea. The sun was already up; she would sit in the garden and make her list for the BBQ later.

Twenty minutes later, Emily was sitting outside with her tea and a slice of toast; she had her list spread out before her and had decided that she would drive to a farm shop she had spotted out on the Bodmin road.

She would buy fresh burgers, chicken, strawberries, cheese, and she would visit the Camel Valley winery and buy some wine. She had been there on a previous trip, just after they had opened; she had recently seen an article about the vineyards and decided this was a good opportunity to visit and take a couple of bottles home.

Emily sat in the garden for an hour before she roused herself; she had her list ready. Everyone had promised to bring additional bits; she would send Max along just before they set off to make sure that Sheila and her two children were still coming.

Emily stood up and stretched; she had really loved this cottage, and although it had been dirty when she arrived, it had potential to be a really secure income for Gwen if she followed the advice she and George had given her and got a decorator in. Gwen had already told Emily not to rush leaving on Friday, as she didn't have another booking till the Sunday. Emily had decided she would leave the place spotless and make sure that the new guest would return. She wanted to help Gwen as she had only known her for six days but had become very fond of her.

Emily went inside and picked up her mobile phone—one text, but it was from her friend Wendy. Emily read it and replied, but felt disappointed; she had expected a text from Simon. She stood at the sink, rinsing her tea mug and plate, musing as to whether last night had been a step too far; when she heard the latch on the gate, she looked up and saw Simon standing awkwardly in the doorway.

Neither spoke; both were waiting for the other to make the first move.

'Hi,' Emily said quietly.

'You OK?'

'Yes, fine.'

'Oh dear, this is so awkward,' thought Emily and turned back to her rinsing.

Suddenly, Simon spun her round. 'Emily, are we still OK? I want to go on seeing you. I need to go on seeing you. Have you thought about what will happen to us after tomorrow?'

Emily lifted her face to his, her eyes shining. 'Oh, Simon, I was wondering with you standing there so uncomfortable that you were about to say it should not have happened. Of course, I want our relationship to continue.'

They sank into a long embrace only to part when Max wandered in. 'Yuk, can't you two get a room?' They both giggled like teenagers.

Simon and Emily stepped apart. Simon glanced at his watch. 'Got to run. Will be late. See you all later.' He gave Emily a quick kiss and ruffled Max's hair as he left.

'Mum, it's OK. Both me and Grace like him. Is he your boyfriend now?'

'Thank you, darling. It means a lot to me to know you and Grace like him. Yes, I think he is my boyfriend.'

Smiling, Emily set about tidying up and sorting out some bits that she wanted to pack in the car later; she would get the children to do their bit that afternoon.

By ten o'clock, they were ready to head off to the farm shop. Max had been along to Sheila and had asked to stay behind with Peter. After a quick chat with Sheila, it was agreed that Max would stay behind, supervised by Sheila's mum, whilst Sheila and Mel would come to the farm shop with Emily and Grace. Sheila didn't own a car, so she had to rely on the local bus service.

The two girls chatted non-stop in the car, whilst Emily and Sheila chatted quietly in the front. Sheila commented that Simon had been around often; she had noticed him the night before when she had put the bins out. Emily blushed.

'I knew I was right,' Sheila smiled triumphantly. 'I told Mum there's an affair brewing there.'

'It's not an affair. Neither of us are attached, nor I hope it's a holiday romance.'

For the rest of the journey, they discussed their own failed marriages.

Once all the groceries were purchased and stowed away in the boot of the car, Emily turned the car in the direction of the Camel Valley and told Sheila what she was looking for. Twenty minutes later, after a slight wrong turn they pulled into the car park of the vineyard. Both women were silent; the view was spectacular. Sheila had never been there before. They followed the signposts to the shop; the two girls asked for crisps and a drink. Emily glanced at her watch and realised that it was twelve thirty.

'No wonder you're hungry. It's lunchtime.' Emily put the drinks and crisps on the counter, and the young lady who was serving handed them to each of the girls.

Both girls took their drink and crisps on to the veranda whilst Sheila and Emily perused the wine and had a few samples. Emily was careful as she had to drive back, but Sheila indulged in quite a few 'tastings'. Emily made her decisions and decided to take a mixture of both white and rosé for the party and a presentation box of their sparkling wine for both her friends back home: Wendy for looking after Bruno and Maria for having to put up with Tania's temper on the first morning she had been away.

Purchases made, they called the girls inside and set off back home. Emily thought that it did actually feel like home, more so than her house in Ringwood; she was always so busy that she never had time to really enjoy her home or her life.

Sheila talked about her job and how much she enjoyed her life in Port Isaac. She explained that the school she worked at was small but excellent. Sheila also posed a question that Emily was trying not to think about herself.

'Would your dad not be better off staying in the home?'

This had been playing on Emily's mind the last couple of times she had rung to check in on her father; she still rang every morning and evening. She was still worried about him, but the staff were confident that he had settled down and was happy—sometimes joining in, sometimes talking in grunts when asked direct questions by staff or other residents.

Emily wanted to wait until she saw him and the home herself on Friday afternoon before she made any decisions; she intended driving straight there. She needed to see it for herself and then make a decision. She would not consult Tania, but she had already decided she would send a cheque to Tania for the full amount of money. There was no way she was going to take anything from her 'bitch' of a sister. Tania always brought out the worst in Emily; she always had and she always would. It did sound as though her dad was more stimulated in the home than he was at the day centre; there he always had the same routine. But it seemed more varied in the home. Emily had worked out that with the cost of the centre, Maria's help, the extra washing, and the time she spent looking after him, it wasn't actually that much more to keep him in the home than at her home, especially if he was happy. It would also be healthier for the children to have their freedom. Emily also had to consider what she would tell the children, and she needed to talk to Simon about their relationship.

By six o'clock, Emily and the children were ready. Peter had already arrived; except for when Max popped home for a quick shower, Max and Peter had spent the day together. George was starting up the BBQ to proclamations from the boys of 'we're starving'.

Gwen arrived next with Mary, closely followed by Sheila, Mel, and her mum, whom Emily had invited earlier. Simon brought up the rear.

Emily blushed as Simon kissed her, and she felt all eyes on her.

Everyone had brought what they had promised and laid it out on the table. Emily suggested that everyone helped themselves to food whilst Simon made sure everyone had drinks.

With the garden bathed in evening sunshine, everyone was in a relaxed mood. Gwen and Mary sat together reminiscing. Gwen took time to tell Emily that she had been a model guest and to offer her a free week in the summer to admire the transformations. Gwen had employed a decorator and was also going to have a new bathroom and kitchen installed.

George winked regularly at Emily whenever he caught her eye; he managed to give her his seal of approval when she went to the BBQ to get a piece of chicken.

'Well, love, you could do a lot worse' had been his statement. High praise from George, who Emily had found out was a man of few words.

Sheila moved from group to group, talking to her neighbours and introducing her mum to both Gwen and Mary, who invited her to join them. The children went off down to the bottom of the garden. At 9 p.m., Mary came over and gave Emily a hug.

'It's a shame, my dear, you're not going to be a permanent neighbour.' Her eyes glinted and Emily could tell she was tearful; she hugged Mary back. It had been nice for Mary to have someone with whom she could talk each day.

'I will keep in touch. I promise to write.' Emily called both children over to say goodbye. Simon came over and draped his arm over her shoulder. Gwen and George moved over and said their goodbyes.

George gave Emily a hug and whispered, 'Invite me to the wedding.' Then he added loudly, 'Leave the BBQ. I will collect it sometime tomorrow.'

Gwen again told Emily not to rush in the morning and that she would see her before she left. George offered to walk Gwen safely to her gate.

Sheila took her cue and rounded up her family and thanked Emily for a lovely day, telling her that she would miss her; it had only been a short time, but they had much in common and had instantly liked each other. She reminded Emily that they would keep in touch.

Emily felt quite emotional as she closed the gate. As she turned back to the garden, she found that Simon had roped in both the children to help put everything either in the bin bags or on the table. There wasn't much left, and Emily popped enough food into the fridge for a light lunch the following day before they left.

By 9.45 p.m., everything was cleared away and Emily had taken Grace up to bed. Max had followed and was already in bed; when Emily popped her head round his door, he was sitting up in bed, reading.

'Why do we have to go home tomorrow if Granddad is not at home with Auntie Tania and the boys?'

Emily sat on the bed and explained that she needed to see for herself that her dad was OK and that the home Tania had sent him to was as good as it sounded on the telephone. Emily looked at Max.

'How would you feel, love, if Granddad likes the home and he stays there?'

Max looked at his mum and spent a few minutes contemplating his answer.

'Well, *if* it is nice and *if* Granddad is happy,' he emphasised the ifs, 'and we are allowed to visit him, then it might be good. It could mean we could have more friends round. Maybe Pete could come and stay with us.'

'You would certainly be able to visit. We all would each weekend.' Emily kissed Max on the head. 'Nite, nite, sleep tight.'

Max grinned. 'Don't let the bed bugs bite.'

'Pete could also come and stay if you wanted him to,' she said as she closed the door.

Emily returned to the lounge. Simon held out a glass of wine. 'You OK?' Emily smiled and sank on to the sofa.

'I'm fine. I can't believe how quickly I have become so fond of this place and the village. I feel so at home here. I've made four good friends and met you. The kids don't want to go home tomorrow and nor do I.' She gave Simon a weak smile.

Simon pulled her to her feet and held her close. 'I don't want you to either. I will miss you.'

Emily lifted her head, and their lips met first gently, then more hungrily. Emily didn't want it to end; she lifted her head, took Simon's hand, and gently pulled him towards the stairs. She put her fingers to her lips, indicating that they needed to be quiet so that the children didn't hear them. Emily was still aware that their relationship would not last and didn't want the children to realise that Simon and she were sleeping together.

In the bedroom, Emily left the light off so that only the moon shone into the room; they slowly undressed each other, exploring and enjoying each other's bodies. Neither was as frantic as they had been the night before. Simon placed light kisses all over her body until she started to moan and lift her body up towards his. Simon reached into his pocket and brought out a small packet. 'I have come prepared tonight.' Emily slid her hands inside his boxers and gently peeled them away; they were both naked.

Friday—Going Home

*E*mily woke up at 5 a.m. with the sun starting to shine through the window. She turned over and looked at Simon still asleep beside her; gently, she placed small kisses on his shoulder. He groaned and reached out for her; it was gone six o'clock before Simon slipped out the back door. He had promised to come back for lunch and see them off. They had talked long into the night in between their love making. Neither of them wanted their relationship to end, and they had decided that a four-hour drive was not an insurmountable problem. Simon had told her about his new job he had taken in Cornwall. Simon had asked her to consider moving to Cornwall as they all loved it so much, if she decided to keep her dad in the home.

Emily had explained how she needed to ensure that her father was settled and happy before she could make any firm plans. Simon was very understanding and had told her how he was happy to wait for her to sort things out.

After Simon left, Emily made herself a cup of tea and a slice of toast, which she decided to take outside. She sat admiring the small garden that only a week ago had been overgrown and in need of some tender loving care. The hedges had been overgrown, the grass had needed mowing, and the borders had been unkempt, but with the joint effort of George and Emily, the garden was tidy. It had so much potential; it sat high up, overlooking the bay. If only the hedge wasn't there, the view would be spectacular. Emily reflected that if she owned the cottage she would remove the hedge at the bottom of the garden to make the most of the view. A nice pergola and some seating could be installed, and the vista could be used to its full potential. The fences also needed replacing. 'But,' Emily told herself, 'it's not yours.' Maybe she could make these suggestions to Gwen later; she seemed really receptive to the suggestions Emily had made so far.

Emily finished her tea, collected up her cup and plate, and went into the kitchen. Simon had texted and suggested that they all meet up in the harbour for lunch. Emily texted back: 'Yes please, looking forward to seeing you soon xx!'

Slowly, Emily started to sort out the last of their things and pack them in the box, ready to go into the car. She didn't have much enthusiasm. She knew that she was about to make some life-changing decisions that involved five people's lives and she would need to have some sort of confrontation with her sister once she got home.

She decided to plate up the leftovers from the night before that were to have been their lunches and drop them off for Mary and Gwen. Once the kitchen was tidy, Emily checked the lounge and bathroom. The pile by the kitchen door was growing as she added her books, a couple of games the children had brought with them, coats and wellies that had not been used, and the fishing nets, buckets, spades, and crabbing lines that they had bought on the first morning. Was it really less than a week ago?

Upstairs, Emily stripped her own bed and added the bedding to the black bag that she had kept ready for washing when she got home. By 9 a.m., she was ready for a shower; she woke both the children and asked them to get dressed and sort out their bits for her.

By 11 a.m., the car was packed; she had dropped off a plate of food for Mary, who had appreciated the gesture and again told Emily how she would miss them. Emily suggested to the children that they might like to go to the harbour. Max wanted to pop in and tell Pete that he would be able to come and stay if Granddad stayed in the home. Emily and Grace went along to drop off the plate of food for Gwen and say goodbye.

Emily spent some time discussing with Gwen about her vision for the improvements to the cottage and garden. Gwen listened to Emily and her visions; she loved her ideas. She reiterated that she wanted Emily to come down in the summer and see the finished results. Emily promised she would and that they would keep in touch with emails and Gwen said she would send photos of the progress. After a slightly tearful goodbye, Emily steered Grace out the gate, and Max joined them to walk down to the harbour.

Simon and Emily sat outside with a crab sandwich whilst the children walked up to the pasty shop; they had become fond of the sweet version, and Emily thought one more wouldn't hurt. It also gave herself and Simon time to say their own private goodbyes.

'I don't want you to leave.' Simon sat holding Emily's hand. 'I want us to be a couple. I have fallen in love with you. I know it's crazy to say it's "love at first sight", but as soon as I saw you, I knew I wanted to know you.'

Emily gently stroked his cheek.

'I want us to remain a couple too. I really do, but I have to sort out my dad first.'

Simon gripped her hand harder.

'I know and I respect that. It's what makes you so sweet. I will phone you tonight and see how things have gone.'

The children returned. 'Can we go, Mum, please?' cried Grace. 'I want to see Bruno and Granddad.'

Simon gave each of the children a hug and ruffled Max hair. 'You look after your mum for me, won't you?'

'Sure, I will. When are we seeing you again?' Max asked.

'Soon.' Simon walked up the hill with them to the car. Gwen and Mary were talking standing by Mary's gate, and Sheila and the two children came out to wave them goodbye. Simon gave Emily a hug and a brief kiss. Everyone said their goodbyes and Emily started up the car.

It took nearly four hours to get back to Bournemouth. Emily had been given directions on how to find the home that morning and she found it easily. Her first impressions were that it looked well kept. The gardens were pretty and flowering; the general appearance was good. Emily and the children got out of the car and walked to the door; there was a notice asking all visitors to ring the doorbell.

A warm-looking lady came to the door. 'Hi, now what makes me think you are Emily and these are your two children?' She held out her hand. 'Dotty. We have spoken several times on the telephone.'

Emily shook Dotty's hand. 'Thank you for all your support this week. It was reassuring to be able to speak to you and check in on Dad. I am going to kill my sister when I get hold of her.'

'I wouldn't do that, dear,' laughed Dotty. 'She doesn't seem to be worth the trouble, if I may say so.'

Dotty took them through the hall, lounge, and out into a large conservatory, where some of the other residents were sitting. The ones with no visitors had care workers sitting with them, some with a couple of residents playing cards and board games, others sitting talking. Her dad was sitting with a kind-looking young care worker who was showing him a book of flowers and pointing out ones they had seen on the recent visit to the gardens.

'Karen, this is Mr Peters' daughter and grandchildren.'

Karen got up and said a shy 'hello' and indicated the seat for Emily to sit down in.

Emily sat with her dad. 'Hi, Dad, how are you?' He continued to look out the window.

She beckoned to the children to talk to him; he always responded to them better than to her.

'Hi, Granddad,' said Grace and leant over and placed a kiss on his cheek.

'Hi, Granddad, how's it going?' Max bent down in front of his grandfather.

He leant forward and took hold of each of the children's arms and then slowly turned his head to look at Emily. She noticed that his hair had been trimmed and he had been shaved; his clothes looked clean and he was pointing to the garden.

Dotty and Karen left Emily and the children with him and suggested that they would bring them some tea and squash. Karen returned with a tray and a plate of biscuits. She had put some tea in a beaker, which was easier for Emily to feed to her dad. When they had finished their tea, Emily turned to the children who were becoming restless.

'I think Granddad would like a walk outside. Shall we push him round the pathway?'

They spent about an hour with him before they went back inside. Dotty had come out and talked to Emily whilst the children played chase around their granddad's chair, reassuring her that he had settled well and that it was entirely Emily's decision as to whether he stayed or not. Emily liked Dotty; she applied no pressure on her to make a decision there and then.

Emily asked if she could have a couple of days to make her decision.

Once they got home and Emily had unpacked the car and put the washing machine on, she made sure that she rang Marie and spoke to her and arranged to meet the following afternoon so that Emily could ask her opinion on what she felt would be a good solution for her dad.

Emily looked around her house; it was not as homely as the cottage had been. It seemed bare, but Emily was impressed at how tidy her sister had left the house, even making up clean beds. But she smelt a rat; it was too tidy!

She went along to Wendy, taking Grace with her to collect Bruno and to thank her for rescuing him. Wendy was pleased to see Emily; she thanked her for the wine that Emily gave her and made a cup of tea whilst she filled her in on the short visit that her sister had made and her departure, including telling her that Tania had not intended to allow her father enough food and drink. Wendy explained that in her opinion it was probably the best thing for her dad that Tania had put him into the home. Wendy also told Emily that she had tidied up for her. 'I didn't want you to come home to the mess she had left the place in.'

Emily left with a happy Bruno and walked slowly down the road; she was seething even more at Tania if that was possible. Tania was a first-class madam who had always got her own way and would continue to do so all the time that James ran around her like a soppy puppy dog.

Emily decided that they would take Bruno for a walk and collect fish and chips for tea. As they returned, they bumped into Mrs Greggs; she looked like she had been waiting for them. It didn't take Emily long to realise that she had been right, as Mrs Greggs quickly told her what she thought of Tania and her deplorable behaviour.

'She was so rude, so uncaring, so stuck up, and so dismissive.' Mrs Greggs was obviously upset by the way Tania had treated her and her father.

Emily reassured her that she had visited her dad that afternoon and had been in regular contact with the home all week; she also explained that she would need to make a decision over the weekend as to whether she was going to unsettle him again and bring him home or not.

By the time both the children were in bed, Simon phoned Emily, who was feeling very emotional. Emily started to cry when Simon told her that he was already missing her. Emily filled Simon in on what had happened at the home and her conversations with Marie, Wendy, and Mrs Greggs. Simon could tell that she was absolutely furious with Tania. They spent time talking about their own personal feelings before saying a reluctant good night and promising to talk the following day.

Emily made herself a cup of coffee and took it upstairs, thinking about what she would say the following morning when she phoned her sister. The next day was Saturday and Emily knew that Tania didn't like being woken up much before ten o'clock, so she intended to phone her and demand to speak to her around nine o'clock.

The Weekend—A Change of Life

*E*mily woke up and looked at the clock; it was only 5.45 a.m., but Emily was wide awake and decided to get up and make a cup of tea. She went into her kitchen and switched on the kettle; she was apprehensive about ringing her sister as she knew she wouldn't win. But she knew that once she had spoken to Tania and got her anger off her chest, she would feel better herself.

Emily stood looking out of her kitchen window; this was a favourite place for her to stand with her early morning cup of tea. Her garden needed attention; she needed to plant bedding plants like she had done in Cornwall for Gwen. Last year with all the extra work with her dad and the extra hours at school, Emily had neglected her garden somewhat. 'If,' she reflected, 'if I decide Dad is better staying in the home, then maybe I can get back to doing my garden this summer.'

By 7.30 a.m., Emily was itching to ring Tania but decided to talk to Simon instead. Simon had a calming effect on Emily's nerves. They chatted for a while before Simon said he was sorry but he needed to get to work, promising to ring later and hear how things went when she did speak to Tania. Emily put the phone down and sat for a while. She already missed Simon and she missed Cornwall; she had loved the cottage. Looking round her home, she realised that she didn't particularly like it much. She had not really liked it when she bought it with her husband, Emily would have preferred a more traditional cottage, but he had insisted on a modern box. Maybe it was time, Emily thought, about moving to something she liked and not making compromises for other people all the time. Emily thought back to all the times during their childhood that she had taken the blame for her sister's misdemeanours, some worse than others. When her father was first diagnosed with his illness, Emily knew that her mother had changed her will, and she knew it was in favour of Emily and the four children and not Tania. Emily knew that it was a way of her mum saying sorry to her for the sacrifices she had made to allow Tania her freedom.

Emily could recall a conversation that she had overheard between her mum and dad when she was about twelve years old. Her mum had noticed a few months previously that a brooch and ring left by her own mother had gone missing. Her mum had been into Fordingbridge that day and had seen in a jeweller's shop a brooch so similar that it had to be the same. She had gone into the shop and had a look; the jeweller was asking £950 and had explained that a young lady had brought it in a few months back. She had been left it by her grandma but didn't like it, so she had decided to sell it to get some money for her college fees; he also had said that he had given £600 for it and a bit more for a ring. It was only in the last few years that Emily realised the consequence of that conversation.

At 8.30 a.m. Emily could wait no longer and dialled Tania's home number.

'Si, 'ello, this is Clifton Peters' house.'

'Hello, please may I speak to Tania? This is her sister,' Emily asked.

'She tell me not to disturb not till house burn down' came back the reply in broken English.

'Who am I talking to please? This is urgent,' Emily tried again politely.

'I am maid. Madam say no talk to anyone please. I need go, sorry.' The lady sounded worried.

'OK. I will ring her mobile, thank you.'

Emily tried Tania's mobile number, but it went directly to answer phone. Emily decided to leave a curt message.

'Tania, ring me back as soon as you can. Your maid won't get you to the phone, very loyal or scared, goodbye.'

Emily was seething; it was obvious that Tania had decided she wasn't going to talk to her. Well, maybe if as they say the mountain won't come to you, she should go to the mountain.

Decision made, Emily ran upstairs; both children were already awake. 'Quick, please get dressed. We are going to visit your cousins.'

Neither of her children argued; they could both tell that she was stressed and knew that they needed to help her. Within half an hour, they were in the car heading towards the M27.

Emily reached the small cul-de-sac where her sister lived within two hours; it was just before eleven o'clock. Tania and James's house stood out; all five houses in the crescent had been built the same, but Tania had added numerous extras to ensure theirs stood out and was different from the others. Tania did not do anything that was not bigger and better than others. Emily had to press the bell on the gate for access. This was the only house with electronic gates, one added extra. A boy's voice answered the call button.

'Hi, Grant, it's Auntie Emily.'

'Oh, hi.' The gates started to open, and Emily drove through up the short auspicious drive. Tania had had a fountain installed in the middle and the drive swept round in a circle so that cars did not have to reverse out when they came in. Emily climbed out of the car and opened the doors for the children to climb out. Grant was standing on the step. Emily gave him a hug. 'Hi, love, is your mum still in bed?'

Grant looked uncomfortable. 'Yes, but I can't disturb her yet!'

'Don't worry. You aren't going to disturb her. I am. Please take your cousins to the kitchen and give them a snack and drink. We had an early start. I won't be long.'

Emily swept up the stairs; having stayed there before, she knew which was her sister's room. Emily threw open the door and switched on the lights.

'What the hell is going on?' Tania struggled to sit up, taking off her eye mask. Tania always slept with a soothing eye mask. God forbid, she had bags under her eyes in the morning; it was all part of her ritual to stay looking young along with Botox and the occasional surgeon's knife.

'Emily, bloody hell, what's the matter? What the hell are you doing here?' Her voice rose to a high-pitched screech.

Emily was furious—she had been all week, but suddenly she could easily have actually hit her sister.

'*You* ask me what's going on?' Emily stood over her sister before continuing, her voice rising to a controlled temper. 'You', Emily pointed her finger at her sister, 'you neglect our father. You can't stand to stay in my house more than one night. You think money can do anything. You are the most selfish of people that I know.'

Emily took a deep breath; she knew she was trembling with rage.

'I have taken the wrap for you for years. I got the blame for things that you did all through our childhood, especially when you stole from our parents, and I ended up with a small wedding because they had spent all their savings on yours, but I will not stand by and allow you to get away with the way you have treated Dad.'

Tania got out of bed and pulled on her silk wrap. 'Emily, calm down. He is in a home, not neglected. He is old. He doesn't know one day from another. He doesn't even know who we are. He has gone gaga. I am not a care assistant.' Tania was annoyed; she could not understand her sister and why she was in such a rage about this. It seemed simple to Tania; that's what homes were for. You put your relatives in them, paid, and then forgot them until you got the call to say that they had died, and you arranged the funeral and stopped the direct debit—simple in the world that Tania occupied.

'Did she let you in?' Tania turned to face her sister; she never ever referred to any of her employees by name, and Emily guessed she didn't even know them. It was always down to James to employ people to help Tania around the house and with the boys.

'Who?' Emily pretended she didn't understand who her sister was talking about.

'That stupid woman that I employ. I told her I wasn't to be disturbed. I will sack her today for this.' Tania was more annoyed that her maid might have let her sister in than her sister's rage.

Emily took a deep breath. 'Your maid did not let me in, and even if she had refused to allow me through the door, she would not have stopped me today!' Emily was still shaking with rage. She had always known that her sister would not understand, but she had thought she would have been more contrite about the situation.

'Emily, don't be so melodramatic.' Tania sank back on to her bed and looked at her clock to make a point; this only incensed Emily more. 'Please, it's early. I need my sleep.'

'You are a selfish, self-centred bitch. You are not interested in how Dad is. You have not rung once to enquire. You have always had your own way. You stole from our parents. I know that, so don't deny it. You left home and then you decided that you needed them to pay for a lavish wedding that they couldn't afford and then you chuck it all in their face because you always made them feel inferior to you. But what I now realise is that we are actually better than you. We have morals. We have looked after each other.'

Emily opened her bag and pulled out a pre-written cheque. She tossed it on to the bed.

'We don't need anything from you now or ever. As far as I am concerned, I don't have a sister. Take your money back and do not bother to contact me in future.'

Tania picked up the cheque and looked at it, then tucked it under the book on her bedside table before pulling the mask back over her eyes and lying down again.

'Shut the door on your way out.'

Emily marched across to the window, threw back the curtains, and then threw open the windows before leaving the lights on and slamming the door as hard as she could on her way out. Emily realised this was petty, but her anger was too raw; she had to make a statement.

At the bottom of the stairs stood a young Asian lady, looking very scared; she was dressed in a black dress with a white apron and a cap. Emily presumed she was the maid. 'Honestly, maid? Who did Tania think she was?' Emily smiled at the woman, squeezed her arm, and told her not to worry. She called the children; both came running out straight away. Emily opened the front door and quickly gave Grant another hug. 'You know where I am if you or your brother ever need me.' With this, they climbed into the car and drove down the drive.

Neither Max nor Grace spoke on their way out, and it wasn't until they reached the M3 that Emily started to speak to the children.

'I am sorry I had to drag you both up here today, but I needed to talk to your auntie Tania.' Emily didn't see a reason to expose either of her children to her row with her sister.

'That's OK, Mum,' Max said. 'Grant said he was really upset that his mum didn't like Granddad.'

'Grant is a lovely boy. Maria said he was very helpful to her and was very kind to Granddad.' Emily was quite touched that Grant was able to see through his mother's selfishness. She realised he was more like his father than Tania; maybe there was hope for him and Adam yet.

To lighten the mood, Emily decided to pull into Fleet Services and buy them all a burger for lunch. As she steered the car off the motorway and into the services, she asked the boys, 'Anyone for McDonald's?'

Both children jumped at the chance to have two in a week; this was unheard of as Emily liked them to eat home-made healthy meals.

'Pleeease,' both children cried in unison.

Emily pulled into her drive at 4 p.m. and realised that she had arranged to meet Marie at four thirty in Ringwood.

'Right, you two, Wendy has said you can go along to her whilst I pop into town and see Marie.'

Neither child argued; they were both tired and would be happy to sit in front of a television and just chill out.

Emily pulled into the car park and put up her parking clock; she grabbed the bag which contained the bottle of wine she had brought back for Marie and headed for Cafe Nero, where they had arranged to meet. The next day she intended to go into Bournemouth and visit her dad again, and she was hoping that after talking to Marie she would be able to make a decision about whether she would bring her dad home or not.

Marie was pleased to see her and very happy with her wine; they sat for an hour and drank two cappuccinos, trying to decide what was best to do. Marie told Emily that she had liked the home when she had visited to take in Mr Peters' tablets, and Emily echoed her thoughts. But Emily still felt guilty that she was contemplating leaving her dad there and not bringing him home. Marie pointed out that life was not going to get any easier, especially now that Emily had met Simon. Marie also pointed out that both her parents would be so pleased that she was happy.

Emily kissed Marie and thanked her for all she had done and for her help with the decision she needed to make. Emily realised that she would probably have a sleepless night. Marie had suggested she ring and speak with Dotty in the morning.

Emily pulled into her drive and walked along to Wendy's house; she knocked on the back door and went straight in. This was what both herself and Wendy always did when they visited each other. 'Hi,' Emily sang out.

'In the lounge,' Wendy called through. Emily went straight into the lounge where the children and Wendy were sitting, watching TV; both children were glued to the screen, and Grace was looking like she would fall asleep.

Wendy raised her eyebrows. 'You look like you need a drink. Wine?'

'Please.' Emily smiled at her friend; she knew Wendy would not start asking questions in front of the children. Emily followed Wendy into the kitchen and closed the door before falling into the chair and taking a gulp of the wine that Wendy set on the table in front of her.

Wendy raised an eyebrow. 'How did it go?'

'Marie was a great help,' she started.

'No, how did it go with Tania? Start at the beginning. The kids said you drove up there this morning, and you were really angry!'

'Angry is probably a mild way to describe how I felt this morning.' Emily took another gulp of wine and started at the beginning.

Wendy only spoke to occasionally call Tania non-complimentary names while she kept Emily's glass topped up.

When Emily had finished telling the whole sorry story, Wendy told Emily, 'She had this coming to her. She really takes the biscuit, and I saw first-hand her temper and the way she spoke to your dad.' Wendy squeezed Emily's hand reassuringly. 'I am glad she isn't my sister. You did the right thing. Your mum and dad would be proud of you.' At this, Emily burst into tears, and Wendy went to the fridge to get a second bottle of wine.

Sometime later, Emily looked at her watch; it was nearly seven and she needed to give both children a snack and get Grace to bed. She stood up and thanked Wendy, calling both children through. 'I will talk to you tomorrow once I have made a decision,' she told Wendy, giving her a hug as she shepherded both children out the door.

It was just after eight when both children were upstairs and in bed, Grace fast asleep and Max reading, when Simon called. As soon as she heard his voice, Emily burst into tears again and repeated the whole saga all over.

Simon listened and made soothing noises as he listened to Emily; he found it hard to understand as he had a close relationship with his own sister. He couldn't understand Tania's behaviour. They talked for a while longer, and then Simon told her that he had accepted the job in Cornwall and would start in three weeks, so he wanted to come up and spend time with her and the children. Both agreed that maybe it would be a good idea to start with if he booked into a local B & B and slowly stayed over once the children got used to having him around. They said a reluctant good night, miss you over again and then for good luck again.

Emily felt much better once she had spoken with Simon and went to bed, happy she would be seeing him by the end of the week. She slept soundly and woke at 7 a.m., knowing what she was going to do.

Epilogue

Emily stood looking around her new kitchen; it had all taken time, but now the cottage was the way she wanted it. Outside in the garden, Grace was looking after her little brother, pushing him up and down the path on his little trike. Ben loved it when Grace had time to play with him, and she adored her brother as did Max. But Max thought it wasn't cool to show it. Grace was eleven years old and was just about to start at secondary school. Emily knew that she was nervous, but so were all her friends and they were all going to travel on the bus together. But Emily also knew that she was excited about the new life she was about to embark on. Max loved secondary school and would keep an eye on his sister, even if only from a distance. As ever, Max was protective of both Grace and Ben, and to some extent, he still protected his mother although he left most of that to his stepfather nowadays.

Emily turned round when she heard a movement behind her.

'Where's Max today?' Simon asked, wrapping his arms around her; they stood together, looking out at Ben and Grace playing.

'I dropped him and Peter into Padstow earlier. They wanted to go and look at the lobster hatchery. They are doing some environmental project for school. They have left it till the last minute. We took their bikes and they are going to cycle back to Wadebridge and then phone me to be picked up about 4 p.m.' Emily loved it that Simon was always concerned about the children, and in the last two years, both children had come to love and respect him and accept him as their stepfather. Grace even called him Dad occasionally, which she knew he loved. Neither had seen their biological father since the day they had left Hampshire; he sent the obligatory birthday and Christmas cards with a cheque, and he paid his maintenance when he remembered. But otherwise he had left them to get on with their lives as he was doing with his own.

Emily had been shocked when six weeks after returning from her original trip to Cornwall she had realised that she was pregnant. Simon and she were still seeing each other and were talking about the future. Emily had decided to leave her dad in the rest home; he had settled in well and was as happy as someone in his condition could be. She had not spoken to her sister since that awful day when she had driven up to confront her for putting him in a home in the first place.

Emily knew she had made all the right decisions. Fate had meant that she had met and fallen in love with Simon. Maybe, fate had a hand in the arrival of Ben. He had cemented the two sides of her family together into one unit.

Emily sighed contentedly as she leant against Simon. At last, she had everything she needed. She stood watching the children in the garden and looked beyond at the view of the harbour, which she never tired of seeing. One of the first things they did when they moved in was to remove the hedge and open up the vista.

Simon had heard six months after Emily had returned to Ringwood through the grapevine when working in Cornwall that Gwen was thinking of putting one of the cottages on the market; he had approached her directly and made an offer on the holiday cottage, which Gwen had accepted. Both Gwen's and George's respective mother and father had died and they had also become an item.

Simon wasn't sure at the time whether Emily would want to move to Port Isaac long term, but having the house would mean they could use it when the children were on holiday and for long weekends, and it would give Simon a base when he was working.

Emily had been over the moon and had suggested that she would sell her own house and that it could pay for renovations. They had rented another holiday cottage over the winter months whilst the extension was done along with full rewiring and new heating, but because the cost of holiday cottages had gone up by more than double in the season they had moved in and continued to renovate until now everything was perfect.

The icing on the cake was the next weekend, when they were getting married with a small reception in a local hotel. Grace, Sheila, and Mel had gone into Truro and found Emily the perfect cream outfit and a little fascinator. George had agreed to give her away whilst Simon had asked Max and his brother to be his best men. Grace and Mel were bridesmaids, and of course, Ben would be the star of the show as pageboy. The only sadness was that this time round neither of her parents would be there to witness this happy occasion. Her dad had passed away six weeks before in the same nursing home. Emily had left him there, not wanting to upset him by bringing him back to the house. She had visited him every Sunday since moving; it took up her entire day, but she had loved both her parents so much. Simon had understood as he too loved his own parents. Simon's parents had welcomed Emily and the children that first summer in France with open arms and had treated Max and Grace the same as their other grandchildren.

Emily had not spoken to her sister since that day when she had driven up and barged in to give her a dressing-down. James kept in touch and had sent them a small present from himself and the boys. He had also brought both the boys down for a weekend the previous summer when Tania had been off on one of her 'retreats'. Emily had invited James and both boys to the wedding, but James had declined. Emily knew this meant that Tania had not been happy that he had come to Cornwall, but Emily was never going to soften her feelings for her sister.

Tania had come to their dad's funeral, but like their mum's, she had left straight away; she had been in touch once with the solicitor to find out what the will had said. He had told Emily that she didn't seem that bothered once she knew that she wasn't going to get anything. Their mother had tied up the will before she died, knowing that all responsibility for her husband when she died would fall on to Emily's shoulders.

Everyone loved Cornwall. Both children had settled in well; they all had a good group of friends and interests. Ben was going to start pre-school in September and Emily was going to work for a few hours in the infant school with a child who had special needs. Emily had always enjoyed her job in Ringwood and had her Level 3 NVQ, so she was well qualified to fill the position when it arose. She was looking forward to getting back to work; although she loved Ben to bits, she found that she needed more. She had always been so busy when the other two were little and then when she looked after her dad; the recent months overseeing the build had kept her occupied, but now she wanted more. Everyone was happy and enjoying life in Cornwall. Emily knew that now her world was perfect.

Lightning Source UK Ltd.
Milton Keynes UK
UKOW03f0255080514

231317UK00002B/139/P